THE CALLOUS CATCHER

1st book in The Gifted Series

EBONY EASTER

For my parents. To the one that gave me the gift of creativity and to the one that told me to use it.

THE CALLOUS CATCHER

PROLOGUE

A nurse named Mrs. Ruby lets free of my wrist and gently shoves me through the metal door. I cough. The medicine they give me is disgusting. It's supposed to keep me alive but it's killing my throat. I squint. The hanging lights glare like the sun. I should know- it was the last thing I saw until I went unconscious.

If you want to hear my story, you need to wait for when I tell the agent waiting for me across the room. I see the empty steel chair waiting just for me. I'd rather run home and cry than sit in that chair. It didn't only scare me, but shouted at me that I would have to tell someone again what happened that day. The day she died.

For now her name is 'she'. Only cause it's too hard to remember her real name. When I fell to the concrete, my brain deleted most things. Except how and when she was killed.

"Miss Wilson," Agent Shelly Clark speaks quietly, as if not to scare me too much. "Are you ready?"

To tell another agent, police officer, friend, or neighbor what happened? No. To go home? Definitely. But I wasn't going anywhere without being questioned to death.

I take a seat. I fold my hands on the cold, steel table where people wept, banged, scratched, and sweat. I wonder which one I was going to do this time.

"How are you feeling?" the agent asks.

I want to tell her to get to the real questions so that I could go home to where people love me and don't demand answers from me. Even if the loss was floating through the house, no one would say a word about it. That's the way I like it.

"Tired," I croak.

She nods at my boring answer. She flips open a tan folder off to her left. Picking up a sharp pencil, I believe she writes down my answer. Either that or the fact I lied. Whatever. Those small questions don't matter to anyone.

"How's your parents?" comes out another boring question.

"Okay," of course I'm going to give her a boring answer. She looks up at me as if to see if I'm playing with her. When Shelly's serious, she looks younger. Her black curls highlighted with golden brown looks perfect. Her eyes are greenish blue. Skinny as a door but absolutely beautiful with a pointy nose, curved ears, and sculptured lips.

"What's wrong?" she gently asks.

"I just want you to get to the questions," I snap, not even wishing to take it back. God how I want to go home.

She presses her glossy lips together. "Alright fine. What do you remember that morning?"

"Nothing."

She slaps her pencil down. "I need you to work with me, Miss Wilson. You pretend not to know anything but that is a lie. I have been told you talk in your sleep, begging someone not to hurt…her."

A headache begins to form dramatically in my head. "I have nothing to tell."

"Which makes you sound guilty," she informs me.

I avert my eyes from her gaze. Ding, ding! We have a winner! I most certainly am sweating to where I could make my own lake and name it 'I'm Innocent, I Swear'.

Shelly leans forward, placing her hand on mine. "I know you'd rather be anywhere but here, but we need to know. You're not helping her, or me, or any other kid out there by being mute."

How would Shelly know anything about helping her? She doesn't know anything about her. Not one thing.

Okay, yeah there are other kids out there that need protecting. I never thought not telling was being unhelpful. But I know a detail that is so unbelievably true that it stings my heart: they aren't ever going to find him.

Why? I haven't figured that out yet. My brain had decided to delete that answer also when he had told me. Right before he took her.

So I might as well prove my innocence. I snap my eyes shut only because the memory comes to me when I'm asleep. Darkness brings out the worst dreams.

It comes back to me in pictures as if I'm shuffling through the scenes.

"Tell me what happens the moment you leave the house," the agent's voice is far away but I still hear her.

A picture of me stepping off the porch comes in view. I was holding her hand, her little, green dress jumping in the air. Her face all smiles.

"Walk down the porch," I say.

I hear pencils move, papers shuffle, feet clap the floor.

"What's your surrounding?"

I hear leaves rustle. Wind blow. Laughs. Mine and hers. Crunch of a leaf from my foot.

"Leaves, trees. Wind," I tell her.

"Was anyone else outside?"

Blank scenes pop up. Empty sidewalks. Empty road. No one in their front yard.

"No one," I answer.

"How long do you walk before..."

I remember her and me playing a game, counting each house we past. One, two, three, four. House seven had a leftover pumpkin in their yard. House fourteen had a beautiful, tall rosebush. House fifteen...we never got to house fifteen.

"We passed fourteen houses."

A sound of a pencil scraping over a paper goes through my ears.

"Miss Wilson, what direction does he come from?" Shelly asks, softly.

I think hard. Squeeze my eyes more. Think Mariam think, I tell myself.

A black figure walks up to us. Couldn't see his face. Can't understand what he tells me. But I call up the moment I yelled at him to get the hell away. My yell makes her cry.

That's when he grabs her.

My nails scratch deadly against the table as I pull my left hand free from Agent Shelly's hold and cover my face with my palms. Tears fall like a leak in the roof.

"I want to stop," I jump out of my seat, my face still hidden.

I hear Shelly's chair squeak back as she stands too.

"Miss Wilson," she speaks slowly, "we need to find him. We need to."

I sniff. "You're not ever going to find him."

"Why not?"

Then it all comes back. Even his face. Almond, curly hair and brown eyes. Tan skin. Big hands. And his deep voice ringing through my ears.

"Because he's just like her," my voice shakes.

Agent Shelly steps away from her chair and up to my face. I can feel her breath on my cold hands. "Like her how?"

"I d-don't know."

"Are you sure?"

I don't say anything, or move my hands off my face.

A soft hand falls gently onto the stitches on the back of my head, where hair is lazily starting to grow over.

"How'd you bust your head?" she asks, moving her hand up and down the stitches.

I remain mute.

"Why weren't you beside her when we found you two?"

My arms are starting to burn. "He pushed me."

"Thirty steps away?"

My hands slap to my side and I step backwards, wanting to get away, very far away. I snap open my eyes and put up my arm, trying to block myself from the agent.

"Leave me alone!" I shout. "I don't know anything! I don't…"

Shelly grabs my wrist and makes me stare into her eyes. "You know why she was murdered. You know why there is something the same between them. What is it?"

I'm crying now, wanting to leave. Wanting to go home. Away from here. Away from the hospital where people treat me like a baby.

She puts her hand on my shoulder. "Tell me how he caused you brain damage, Miss Wilson. We need to know what were up against. Please try to remember."

Remember? I've been trying my hardest to forget and now I need to remember. Great.

Slowly, my eyes close.

I see a picture. He grabs her up. I hear her scream. Keep going, I tell myself. I pull on his arm to give her back to me. He slaps me in the cheek. It stings. I tumble onto a bunch of crumbled leafs.

Don't stop, I think. Almost there.

I watch him run, his black cloak floating in the air. She's crying and screaming so loud that I can't believe the neighbors can't hear her. I climb back onto my feet, determined to get her back. My feet crunch the leaves I run over, trying to reach him. He was far, house twenty-three maybe. But I can run. I've been running for years. I find my speed, moving faster than I've ever had in my entire life. I was right behind him. I could almost see the tears on her face. A picture of him jumping onto the road flashes past my eyes. But still, I had run after him, going onto the road as well. I was six steps behind him when he lands back onto the sidewalk with her struggling in his arms. I see a flicker of light to my left. Turning my head, I see it-

My hand jumps onto Agent Shelly's arm. "A car. A car," I repeat.

With my left hand still covering my left eye, I try to remember. Remember, remember. Focus, Mariam.

I see myself on the ground, the back of my head open and bleeding. Another light comes and goes. The car is gone in a moment of seconds. Not down the road but suddenly out of view. Vanished. Then my eyes find the sun. The heat burns. It burns and stings. Then I black out.

My eyes open and I move my hand away from my face. Agent Shelly sits me in my seat but it didn't help my constant shaking.

"Who was driving the car?" she asks, her pencil positioned over her paper.

"No one."

"No one?"

"The car was driving by itself because…"

"How did the car end up there?"

I shudder. I really didn't know. "It came out of nowhere."

"What do you mean?" she asks, confused.

I swallow. "A-a light flashed to my left and then the car appeared."

"Out of nowhere?" she asks.

"Y-yes. And leaves with a flashing light." I'm not crazy, I thought.

Agent Shelly clears her throat and looks up at me. "Thank you. I think that's all we need. Do you have anything else to tell me?" she asks.

I shake my head. I just want to go home.

Agent Shelly stares at me for a whole minute.

I roll my eyes, something I haven't done in days. "What?"

She pushes her lips together. "Do you remember her name?"

Don't answer.

"Do you remember who she is to you?"

I nod.

"The only way you're going to forget this all is to know and accept who it happened to."

I nod again. Not for agreement, just to do something.

"Can you say it?"

I do nothing.

"Can you think it?"

Think it, I thought. Think it. Think it.

He killed her. She meant everything to me. She changed my life. But then he destroyed that. Destroyed her.

Her.

She.

My sister.

My baby sister.

Oh my God.

She was only three years old.

CHAPTER 1

3 months later

"I swear he's checking you out," my friend, May Watson, whispers in my ear.

I take a peak over my lunch bag to look. Oh my God, he is.

Dillon Evans.

Cutest boy ever is checking me out. Right across the lunch room he's staring at me with those sunset eyes. Our eyes meet. And then he smiles, dimples flashing. Frogs leap around in my stomach. I was so shocked I couldn't smile back.

His gaze falls onto his plate, showing me the view of his black hair. I wanted to scream. Instead I shake my head and pretend he's not there.

May nudges me with her elbow hard, to where her blonde waves bounce around. "I told you he was lookin'."

"I don't see the big deal about Dillon," Ashley Field, the other friend in the group, speaks up. "Why don't you just go up and talk to him. He used to be your best friend, right?"

I slowly start to nod. He *did* used to be my best friend. We met in first grade and turned buds immediately. I've had a crush on him for, like, ever and he had a crush on Nelci Griffin since third grade when she gave him his own, special valentine card. The girl he's sitting by. Holding hands with. Her shiny, dyed black hair on *his* shoulder.

Yes, they're a couple. Congratulations. They've been a couple ever since seventh grade. Four years. That's like four more anniversaries that we could have had together. You know, when we do date.

Dillon's now in the more important crowd. Good for him. You know, if I was his mom I would be *so* proud of him. So very proud that he ditched his first best friend for a girl who probably stuffs her bra and likes to prey on the weak. How could a mother be any more proud?

I clench my teeth together. I am so far done with being mad at Dillon. It's Nelci who's my enemy.

Anyhow, it's not like I never tried to talk to him. Freshman year, I snuck up to his room through the window. But I found him making out with Nelci. And then my foot slipped and I fell down in his mom's flower bed. I would love to tell you he jumped out of his window and asked me if I was okay. I would tell him no and he would carry me home and wrap up my sprained ankle with his shirt. At the end he would kiss me good night.

Well…there's your reason why I stopped believing in fairytales. And also the first time I had to lie to my parents about my injury. (I told them I fell out of a tree. See, not completely a lie. I did fall. It just wasn't exactly a tree that I fell out of.)

Until this moment I found him staring at me. Maybe there isn't fairytales, but there sure is good luck.

I almost slide off the bench when May nudges me again.

"You should go talk to him," she dares with her little girly smile. May has way too long, wavy, blond hair. Her eyes are a sparkle blue on her light-colored skin completed with perfect eyebrows and lengthy eyelashes.

"And say what?" I ask. I, on the other hand, have black hair in longish braids and deep brown eyes on my dark skin. I have a tight bone structure in my face and muscles from volleyball, soccer, and basketball.

"Why the hell are you ignoring me," Ashley rolls her light brown eyes like she can't believe I don't know how this world works. She captures a piece of her fake black hair and hides it behind her ear. She takes out her mirror and inspects the new eyeliner she smeared on her chocolate skin this morning.

Ashley Field is not one of those girls you mess with. Not even talk about. She could kill you with her weave. Not that I like friends that can kill using weaves, but she gives awesome advice. At least I think she does.

"I am not going to walk over to that table and just ask him why he's ignoring me," I said.

"Why not? Show Dillon that your tough and you shouldn't be treated like this. He might actually find it attractive," Ashley adds, dropping her mirror back in her bag.

"No-"

"Look, look! He's getting up," May says, pulling on my arm, excited.

Ashley gives me a wicked smile. "Would you rather ask him in front of ten stuck-up people or while he's going to the bathroom?" If Ashley wasn't my friend, I would've tried to sock her.

May shoves me off the bench. Luckily I have great balance and steady myself before I fall face-first into an ugly hamburger left to rot on the floor. I stand straight and smooth down my shirt and pull up my jeans. Slowly, I take a deep breath and let it out just like how Ms. Bell, my therapist, taught me to do. Most of the time I don't listen to what she says, but this breathing exercise I know works. It helps, at least some.

Passing the popular table I can hear them laughing about something. They're always laughing, as if trying to make everyone feel jealous. I hate to say that they are doing a good job at it.

I push through the cafeteria doors, almost anxious to get up to him. But when the doors close behind me, I find the hallways completely empty. He couldn't have gone into the bathroom that fast. I mean, unless he needed to pee really bad. I might as well go back in and-

"Mariam?"

I jump, scared out of my wits. I switch around with my hands up as if prepared to put up a fight.

Dillon stood a couple of inches away, hands in his locker, eyes on me. I suck in my breath. Second time in four years, four months, one week, and six days I found his eyes on me. It felt so good to be noticed by him again, by those bright, hazel eyes.

I didn't realize I was daydreaming until he calls my name again.

"Oh yes!" I shout.

He chuckles and takes his hands out of his locker to smooth back his perfect, black hair. "What were you daydreaming about this time?" he asks, grinning. "Being a lawyer or going home to play with your Barbie's?"

I make a shy smile than wipe it off my face. "I gave away all my Barbie's in seventh grade."

"Even Madison, your favorite?"

I gasp. I can't believe Dillon actually remembered Madison. She was my favorite Barbie. But I gave her away when Dillon gave me away. She held to many memories of him.

My Barbie's would always be scattered all over the floor when he used to come over. But Madison would be placed on the bed comfortable and neat. I would beg Dillon to play Barbie's with me, not allowing him to leave until he did. He agreed each time. Just to be nice, I would let him use Madison. He would dress her up in funny clothes far from matching. Sometimes he would put the pants on her chest and shirts on her legs. He would put her hair in screwed-up ponytails. It always made me laugh; I really liked it.

When he left me that was the first thing I threw at the wall. I bit off her head and burned all the clothes infected by his hands. So I didn't exactly give her away, unless "to the trash" is included.

"*Mariam*, you still there?"

I clear my head and look up to see Dillon standing right in front of me.

"You...you should get back to your friends," I tell him.

He looks confused and almost a little sad. "Did I do something wrong?"

I stare at him. "No..."

I turn around to walk away. He catches my arm. But I don't turn to look at him. The way his hand felt on my arm told me that he was going to say something I'm not goanna want to hear.

"I'm sorry about your sister."

But I didn't expect that to come out of his mouth.

Our eyes meet and my arm drops to my side. "How'd you know?" I whisper.

I knew it was a stupid question the moment it leaves my mouth. Half the world knows. A girl murdered on the streets with her sister by her side that earned brain damage from having her head smashed into the ground is a story definitely earning a spot on the television, internet, and newspaper and wherever else they put depressing stories like that.

Dillon shrugs, casually. "Just because we don't keep in touch, doesn't mean our parents do the same."

A safe answer.

He steps even closer. "Why didn't you just tell me yourself?" he asks.

He wasn't touching me, but I could feel his body heat. He was so close that if I stick out my tongue, his face would be an inch from it. I could smell his cologne. It smells different than what he used to smell as a kid- mud and oranges.

"I-I wanted t-to but-" I try.

The bell rings through the hallways, demanding everyone to go back to class. Dillon steps away from me as people push through the lunch room doors. They crowd between us and behind. I watch, with no expression, as Nelci snatches his hand from his side and pulls him toward their next class. She gives me a glare when she catches me watching them.

She was lucky I was too shocked to give her one back.

I walk along the sidewalk, after school, passing honking cars and other students. I slip through big groups of people, invisible to them. Though they're only pretending they don't notice me, just think I'm another random student. I know they are, because once I go past them, I can feel their curious eyes tickling my neck. I'm sure what's going through their head is something close to, "There goes the girl with brain damage and the murdered sister."

I stop by the black car parked at the side of the street and the driver in his black suit opens the back door for me. I get in and snap on my seatbelt. The driver gets inside and soon the school is behind us.

Hamptons is my home. It's where I was born, where I am raised, and where I'm supposed to spend the rest of my life as a lawyer. The lawyer part doesn't bother me. That's been a dream for I don't know how long. It's *staying* in Hampton that bothers me. I'm rich and spoiled. I admit it. And I'm unbothered by people not as wealthy as my family, but a girl like me wants privacy. Not parties every holiday at our house, or my parents trying to hook me up with a doctor, and not forced to be perfect in school so I'll look like the golden child. I'd feel so much better if I didn't have any of that to think about.

The car stops and I shove out a sigh. The driver lets me out and I hold onto the straps of my backpack. To keep my hands from shaking maybe. Not because I'm scared. But because I always get frustrated here. I thought that agent's question three months ago was torture. Ms. Bell is worse.

I jog up the fifty white steps and open the mirrored doors into the tall building. I pass up the gray haired lady at the counter to get to the elevators. In the long hallway beside the elevator you can hear married couples yelling and failing at trying to reconnect their love life. What's even worse is that you know they're lost and reconnecting is a long, *long* way from now.

I ride to floor three. Two doors down and I'm knocking nicely like I *want* to be here. The door opens and I move my feet forward.

I smell lavender the minute I walk in. The essence is set on the wall beside Ms. Bell's photos of her two sons. The walls were painted a light yellow with random pictures of strangers smiling. I'm sure they're strangers to Ms. Bell as much as they are to me. She tried the nice vibe theme but it obviously hasn't been working on me. I've been coming here for two months once a week and all she has gotten out of me is my favorite candy (chocolate, if you really care). Big achievement Ms. Bell.

"Sit down and let's talk."

How many times has she said that to me?

I sit down on the white couch and set my backpack on my lap. I watch her watch me.

She put her glossy, black hair in a cheerleader ponytail and pat on more blush than usual this time. Her freakishly blue eyes make her baby doll face too noticeable and her height is pretty decent for a thirty year old. I maybe could like her as a person. You know if she could ever stop pestering me with personal questions.

"How was school?" she asks, sitting in a silver chair across from me, a glass coffee table the only thing between us.

"Painful," I speak truthfully. Except the part with Dillon. Never painful with Dillon.

"And why is that?"

I shrug. "Boring teachers teaching you boring things that you'd never use in the future."

"What about health class. You'll need that information in the future won't you?"

"Not if you plan to live under a rock."

"Is that your plan, Mariam? To live under a rock?"

My mouth falls shut. Somehow the conversation always leads to my future or past. And I never answer either of them entirely.

"Living under a rock would be a very simple life Ms. Bell."

She rolls her lips in and crosses her legs. "Tell me Mariam…are you afraid to die?"

I completely freeze. This is a new question. "What?" I barely whisper.

"Death, Mariam. Is that your greatest fear?"

"Course not," I gasp.

"It's okay. Being afraid of finding out what happens in the afterlife is rational. Lots of people are."

"But I'm not one of them."

"My father was. He still is actually. Sometimes the fear is so deep and hidden that you don't even know it's there, Mariam."

"But I'm not afraid! I'm scared that I'm not protecting my family good enough, not death…"

Ms. Bell's looking at me very closely and it just dawns on me that I answered one of her questions. What am I afraid of? That was the first thing she asked me when I stepped into her room. I had answered flying pigs and laughed because I was nervous. That was the last time she asked me that.

This day is turning out to be very bad.

"Mariam, look at me."

I look at her.

"It's not your duty to watch over your family. It's not."

But after having one of them die because you failed at helping them, it changes to be.

"Since we're on the family subject-"

I roll my eyes.

"-let's talk about your brothers and sister. How are they doing?"

"Fabulous," I said.

"That's nice, but I want to know how *you* think they're really doing."

I sigh very loudly because I want Ms. Bell to know that I'm frustrated. My heads already hurting and I haven't even been here that long.

"I really don't know. It's not like I can read minds."

"Have you asked them? Maybe the youngest- he needs someone to talk to."

"Yeah, your right. I think him and me should switch," I suggest.

Ms. Bell shakes her head and scratches her arm. "Do me a favor Mariam."

"Yes?"

"Ask them when you get home. For me, just go in one of their rooms and talk to them. You might help them in a way you didn't know you could."

I stare down at my hands and bite my lip. "I'll think about it," I mutter.

I swing on my backpack and stand up.

"One more thing, Mariam."

I sit back down, uncertain.

"How are those dreams you've been having?"

It feels as if someone punched me in the gut. I choke a little bit then quickly try to transform the sound into coughing. I pretend to be confused.

"What dreams?"

Ms. Bell seems to buy it. "The one's you keep having every night."

"I told you they've stopped coming four weeks ago," I said, going stiff and telling myself that screaming out loud will probably not help my case.

Ms. Bell licks her lips. "Well I was just wondering if they came back. They left so suddenly."

"Yep," I say eager to end this conversation. I get up and move toward the door.

My therapist stands up also. "Mariam, I just want you to be happy."

I open the door.

"Please-"

And then shut it in her face.

I've never left that place so mad before.

Truth is I still get those dreams. Those nightmares. I get them every single dang night, even when I take a nap. It's like I can never sleep peacefully.

It's quiet in the car as the driver takes me towards home. We drive past an elementary school and I see little kids jumping. I feel a hurtful pinch in my heart. I can't stop myself from thinking it. Thinking that she could've been one of those kids. The kids having fun and living life. If only…

Shut up. *Shut up*, Mariam, I thought. Do not bring her up again. She's out of your life. For*ever*.

By the time the guard opens the gate for us, I'm on the verge of screaming and tearing out my hair. I tell myself to breathe in and out. This time it hardly helps. Walking inside my house, I'm sure I look constipated. I take off my shoes, my feet clapping onto tile. I look in front of me at the two flights of stairs. I'll have to run up both of them to make it to my room.

On the third floor is the grand master bedroom. The first floor, where I am, is the kitchen, family room, living room, and dining room. The second floor holds lots of random rooms, like a small gym, theater, and my parents study room. There is also my room, my brothers, Jamui and Saultan, and my sister, Islamiat. There's a library on the second floor too, but no one really goes in there. Actually, I haven't been in there since I was eight.

I feel like running up the stairs, seeing if I could make it to my room, and let out a frustrated scream. But the woman my parents hired to watch over us and cook us meals and occasionally clean while they're gone working (like always), walks around the corner from the kitchen. We call her "the nanny". I knew screaming into a pillow will have to wait till later.

"Mariam," the nanny says, already grabbing my shoes out of my hand, "come into the kitchen, there's cookies."

Politely, I follow her into the kitchen, dropping my backpack by the staircase. We move through a short hallway with the walls painted gold. We walk down two steps that land us directly in the kitchen between the fridge and stove.

Sitting at the dinner table are my siblings, Saultan, Islamiat, and my older brother Jamui. Jamui's playing with his phone, ignoring everyone. He has been ever since she died. She changed his life the most.

"Get some cookies," the nanny leads me to the table.

I grab a cookie, not determined to sit down, to just go upstairs and finish stressing out. But the nanny pushes a chair back for me to sit and I obey.

"Hi Mariam," Islamiat greets me.

I smile at her and Saultan. I peek at Jamui. His eyes are on his phone. Like that would make him invisible.

"Hi Jamui," I said.

Wow. Not even a nod with his head. He needs to get over the fact that she's gone. Everyone else has. Plus, he's supposed to be strong for Saultan and Islamiat. The only thing he's being is weak. Saultan needs a role model.

Without thinking, I drop my stupid cookie on the table and run out of the kitchen. I snatch up my backpack from beside the staircase and race up the stairs. I find my room quick and lock myself in.

I finally get to scream.

CHAPTER 2

It's not that I didn't study on purpose. I was just too busy trying to keep my hair on my head.

I had screamed all night. Then cried. And screamed some more. The worst part, it did no good at all. It almost made everything a lot worse.

I'm sitting in Algebra 2 class and I have one problem. There's a test and I didn't study. Not that I always do- actually I don't at all- but I need my grades to stay high so that I can get into volleyball. And that's not exactly going to work out if I have an F. I also realize I don't have a pencil when Mrs. Olden smacks the test onto my desk. I raise my hand.

She rolls her eyes. "Yes?"

"I don't have a pencil," I answer.

"Well, *find* one."

I sigh, frustrated. I look on the ground. None. I search the empty desks. None. Then I look at the full stacks of pencils on the teacher's desk. How selfish of her. Well if I don't have a pencil that means I can't take the test, right?

Then I feel something fall between my legs. I look down, curious. A *pencil*. I inspect the classroom, looking for the student who had thrown it. Each kid is either staring at their test or into space. I pick it up from between my legs. It's new, sharp, and smooth in my fingers. As I write my name, I feel the weight of my strength scrapping off lead. The pencil feels so weak that it could break any second. I silently beg it not to.

It lives through the whole test. And when the bell rings, I drop it inside my backpack.

Leaving the classroom, May jumps next to me. We walk through the hallway, everyone pushing through us to go home. Some jocks up ahead shout how happy they are that it's Friday. I smile a little even though they're totally annoying.

"I never asked," she said. "How'd it go?"

"How'd what go?"

"You know," she wiggles her eyebrows. "D-I-L-L-O-N."

I roll my eyes. I know it's her way to try to keep him a secret, but I think the whole school can spell.

"Uh nothing," I lie.

"Nothing like all-we-said-was-hi, or nothing like I'm-not-going-to-tell-you-because-it's-too-big-of-a-secret?"

"Uh…nothing," I say again and try for a laugh, but it comes out all weird.

I find my locker and do the combination. I get it right the second time. I open it and watch as a red note floats out. May snatches it up from the ground. I could've stopped her, but it would have been no use.

It seems like it only takes her a second to read it before she starts "oohing" and raising her perfect eyebrows at me, her blue eyes wide.

"I don't think *he* thought it was nothing," she giggles.

I snatch the paper out of her hand, my mind racing with thoughts of what he wrote.

Mariam, we really didn't get to catch up that much. Let me take you out tomorrow night. Answer the door if it's a yes.

-D.

Tomorrow. Saturday. At night. With Dillon. Alone. What does that mean? Is it a date? No, it can't be- he has a girlfriend. And they seem pretty close. So…it's more like a get-together or a way to spark back up our friendship. Right?

"O.M.G. this is so great," May exclaims. "Okay, give me a piece of paper. I just *have* to write down your outfit."

"May, it's not-" I try.

"Please. Let me do this."

I sigh and turn back to my locker. I find a scratch of paper sitting there, one I didn't notice. One that I'm pretty sure was not there before.

I pick it up. Almost immediately, it crumbles to little pieces. They fall to my shoes. They lay there as if dead, leaving nothing in my hand.

"Okay, that was weird," says May. "No worries, just give me another one."

Then my head starts to buzz, to where it even hurt my ears. I wanted to grab onto them and scream but I don't want to scare May. She gets sensitive when she witnesses pain. Instead, I shut my locker, grab onto my backpack, and tell her I need to run, apologizing.

I pace out the front doors of our school and run down deformed steps. I push through a couple of freshmen girls gossiping. I just want to find my driver. I keep walking. My head feels like it's going to fall off any second now. Where the heck is the car?

Right behind me, a car honks, making me jump with fright. I turn around to find a red truck veering behind me. In the driver's seat is Charmaine Robinson, smiling and laughing. Knowing if I don't get in the car she will never leave, I jog to her and jump inside. When I close the door, Charmaine's still having a good laugh. I ignore her and lock my seatbelt. She drives away from the curb and towards where I live. Her eyes are getting watery for laughing way too much.

"Could you have been anymore scared?" she chuckles.

I look at Charmaine, but my head hurts too much for me to smile. Her long, black hair is up in a faultless ponytail, showing her caramel colored face. Black sunglasses shields her calm brown eyes, making her look a lot older than seventeen. She has a short, sky blue dress on that squeezes her sides and forces her to breathe slowly. I haven't seen her in such a long time. She's two years older than me but we've known each other for a very long time. She looks even more gorgeous now. She doesn't go to my school and she's always out partying or shopping or something that doesn't allow her to stay by the phone at home, that I have to wait for her random visits to see her. Like now.

"Charmaine, you know I have a driver," I remind her.

"Oh that guy. Yeah, I sent him home. He's not as fun as me."

I rest my hands on the dashboard but they fall onto a magazine. On the cover is a girl only wearing a bra and thong lying on top of a black and red motorcycle. I look around the inside of the truck and just notice the bag of chips beneath my feet, fake set of small breasts hanging from the rearview mirror, and soda cans crowded in the back seat.

"Uh Charmaine, who's car is this?" I ask, digging my hands inside my white sweat jacket.

"My boyfriends," she grins as if we are riding in the top car.

"Which one?"

She rolls her eyes. "What are you trying to say, Mariam?"

"I think it's pretty obvious. It rhymes with dough."

She laughs. "Don't be jealous."

"Trust me, I'm not," I said, as we turn the corner to my house. I wave at the guard and he gives me a small smile. He allows the gate to slid open.

"Give me a pen and I'll write down my last boyfriend's number. I think you'd like him. Believe me, he'll get you out of your comfort zone."

"Pen..." I whisper to myself. The memories at what just happened at school come back to me quick. How the pencil appeared in class when I needed it, but how it was so weak, like not made of wood at all. And when May asked for paper. I was positive there was none in my locker, but there it was. And then how it crumbled to pieces in my hand. The weird part is, when I had walked away from my locker, I swear the crumbled paper had disappeared. And there was a light that took it away.

Something small taps my thigh. Before I could look down, Charmaine grabs it from my lap.

"Thanks," she says, holding up a pen. "I'll write it on your palm."

The yellow pen begins to slowly bend in her hand. It hangs over the back of her hand, as if wanting to break but can't.

"Hey it must be one of those bendable pens," Charmaine suggest, parking in front of my house.

Yeah, if they had ever made bendable pens.

Suddenly, I feel worse than I ever did. It feels like my brain's trembling in my head. My hands are quivering violently, to where I want to bite on them to stop the shaking. And my stomach- it's the feeling when you're on a rollercoaster and going down a big dip. My heart beats twice as fast. My feet feel close to numb and my legs are almost paralyzed. As if that wasn't enough, I need to throw up. I mean, I need to throw up *now*.

I clutch my backpack and open the truck door, tripping out onto my driveway. I run towards the front door and fumble with my keys, my mouth clamped shut. Then my mom opens the door from the other side, her car keys in hand to leave. I push through her, ditching my backpack and belongings. My legs are giving up on me. I crawl up the stairs, one hand over my mouth. My brain bangs into the side of my head, making me almost scream out in pain.

I find my room only with my left eye. My right eye had closed, feeling like it is glued shut. I run into my bathroom limping. My right leg was completely out of reach. I grab onto the sink as I try to reach the toilet. It's too far and I know one more step would kill my left leg too. My left eye is already closing up on me. Desperate, I move my hand away from my mouth and open it up over the sink. Liquid and indescribable food tumbles out. The contents from my mouth crowd together in the sink. I stare at my disgusting throw up (when is it ever beautiful), at all the colors, unable to move. Then I barf once more, for a shorter time and only one thing slips out of my mouth: blood.

"Mariam?" someone calls from my room.

My left leg loses strength, dropping me to the cold floor. My head bangs on the ground. My legs and arms don't move, literally paralyzed. An invisible fist punches me in the stomach. My brain kicks my forehead. I see my mom run in and fall to the ground beside me.

My left eye closes.

"Mariam, look I drew," she says, holding up a piece of paper with her stubby fingers. The paper had colorful, crazy lines drawn all over it.

"It's beautiful," I hear my voice say. Where am I?

She's sitting in a small chair coloring on a wooden desk. The room she's in is completely white. No color except the desk and the numerous crayons on it. No light bulbs but light is shining from somewhere.

She moves her hands around the crayons searching for one she seems not to have. She stops looking and holds her hand open.

"Blue," I hear her whisper.

A perfectly, blue crayon appears in her right palm. Just out of nowhere. Naturally, she starts drawing with it, creating random lines.

"How did you do that?" I ask, suspicious.

She looks up at me and smiles, a smile that doesn't look like any of her own. The lights turn off. It looked like my eyes are just closed, but I know I'm still in the dream. I can still feel her. And someone else.

She screams.

"Sis!" I shout.

Nothing.

"Are you okay?"

"You're never going to find me!" his voice rumbles.

My sister screams again, and this time, I scream with her.

My eyes open. I look around myself. I'm in my room, in my bed. My window is open, allowing in freezing air. I move my toes and fingers- not paralyzed. I pull my feet out from under my covers and crack my back. My breath smells bad but mostly I'm thirsty. I walk into my bathroom barefoot with my normal shirt and jeans still on and hang my mouth under the faucet. The sinks clean. The nanny probably had washed it. I wonder what she was thinking while she scrubbed the food and blood out of the sink.

I walk back into my room and slam my window closed. It's a little after dinnertime, the sun is almost gone. I can already find the moon.

I dig my feet into my blue slippers I got for Christmas two years ago from Jamui. You know, when he *was* talking. I open my door and step out into the hallway. Instantly, I notice that there's a visitor. As quietly as possible, I stop at the railing of the stairs and peek down.

What is she doing here? What, does she need *more* information out of me?

Shelly Clark, the agent that made my nightmares worse, is standing in my house by the front door, speaking with my mom. She looks oddly the same only because she looks like one of those people who would change their look often.

My mom and she are on the brick of arguing.

"She doesn't feel well," my mom tells her. "You can come back another time."

"But I need to talk to her now," Shelly snaps. "It's very important."

"What exactly is it about?"

"It's hard to explain. But your daughter will know what I mean if I talk to her."

My mom shakes her head. "No. I said she is sick."

"I wonder why," I hear the agent whisper and notice the sarcasm at the edge.

She looks up at my mom. Actually down, sense Shelly's like four inches taller than her. "Alright, I'll go. I am sorry to have bothered you, Mrs. Wilson."

"Thank you."

"And I hope she gets well," she said as my mom opens the front door for her. Slowly, the agent points her eyes at me. I hold my breath, waiting for her to call my name. She doesn't. She walks out the door without another word. My mom closes it behind her and locks it, then disappears into the kitchen.

Curious, I run back into my room and lift open the window. I flip off my slippers and pull on my tennis shoes. I grab onto the white pole outside of my window and jump out of my room. I wrap my legs around the pole to get ready to slide to the bottom. Don't worry; I have done this hundreds of times. I slide down smoothly, my feet smacking the grass at the end. I run through the backyard, trying to get to the front of the house. I run past the pool and hot tub and around the shed. I jump over Mom's square flower bed and push through the black gate that allows me to enter the front yard.

And there she is. Leaning against her small car and staring at me, as if just knowing I was going to come out to see her.

She watches me as I walk up to her. I watch her too. There's something different about the way she looks at me. Like she knows something that she's begging to tell.

"Hello Ms. Wilson," she greets me when I get close enough.

"What are you doing here?" I ask, suspicious.

"Looking for you."

"I know but…why?"

She opens the passenger door of her car. "Feel like a car ride?" she asks.

"Not from you," I snap. "Look can you just tell me what you want?"

She looks around where we are. "We don't know who might be listening."

"What?"

"How are you feeling?"

"Hey, don't change the subject," I say, getting in her face.

"Who might be listening?"

"You felt like you were dying today, didn't you?"

I step back. "How would you-"

"Ms. Wilson, if you don't use it right, you could kill yourself."

"If I don't use what right?"

"Your gift," she answers. "It's very important that you use it right."

I begin backing away. "Look crazy lady, I don't know what the hell you're talking about."

"No, I think you do."

The thought just couldn't stop from coming to my head. Is she talking about what happened to me today?

"Ms. Wilson…" she steps towards me.

"No, leave me alone!" I shout.

I turn around and run back to my room. I run past the flower bed, shed, pool and hot tub, and finally climb through the window and into my room. I close the window once I get inside. I sit down on my bed and shut my eyes.

The only thing bugging me is the fact that I know she is right. And something, something *way* deep down in me, is telling me to trust her.

Yes, it's telling me to trust the woman who doubled my nightmares and made them all worse.

CHAPTER 3

"What if he kisses you?" May asks.

"Then he kisses her," Ashley says.

I try to ignore them both, but it's hard because they're making me feel giddy and scared. And that's not what I want. I keep telling myself that it's just Dillon. I've been out alone with Dillon lots of times. Maybe not on a date but we've been to the park together and each other's houses when our parents are in the other room. That counts at being alone. I mean, how different is a date from hanging out? There'll still be people there.

Wait, it's not a date. It's not. Yeah, keep telling yourself that, says the evil me in my head.

Shut up.

Me, May, and Ashley do this all the time- stay over at each other's house when were on a date (it's not a date!) so that when we'd come home, we could gush to each other all about it. Easier than waiting till the next day or calling them.

"But really, what are you going to do if he does *kiss* you?" May asks again, walking behind me as I stare at myself in the mirror.

"What is she supposed to do, May?" Ashley asked, pulling up her legs on the chair by my desk.

She shrugs, smiling, and flops down on my bed. I walk over to my window and open it wide. Cold air breezes in. I can't believe it's Saturday already. It seems like just any hour ago I was throwing up my last meal and cursing at Shelly in my head for reappearing in my life unwanted. I turn to my two friends and open my arms.

"So, how do I look?"

They check out my blue dress that ends at my knees, my straightened black hair, and white flats.

"I like it!" May approves.

"You don't think it's too much?"

"No."

"Yes," Ashley says with a nod of her head. She opens her mouth to explain. "I have never seen you wear a dress before. Not even a skirt. Is Dillon really worth it?"

"Don't listen to her, she hasn't been on a date since freshmen year," said May.

"It's not a date," I tell them just as the doorbell rings through the whole house.

"Oh sure," Ashley rolls her eyes.

May grabs my sweater and white handbag and pushes it into my hands.

"Have fun on whatever-you-want-to-call-it," she whispers in my ear.

I suck in my stomach as I walk out of my bedroom and down the flight of stairs. I clutch onto my purse as if someone is planning on stealing it. I try not to blink my eye as I feel an eyelash disturb it. I don't want a tear to fall and ruin my eyeliner May had delicately smoothed on. And the fact that I feel like tripping in *flats*, frightens me.

Once I step off the stairs, I just about want to stab my eyeball, fling off my shoes, and throw my purse at the wall. But the knock at the door calms my nerves.

I pat down my hair and ignore the eyelash as I open the door. I smile until I notice his outfit and the gift in his hands and realize that I might be wrong. That we actually might be going on a *date*.

He's dressed in nice, blue jeans and clean, black shoes. He's wearing a white shirt and leather jacket. Around his neck is a silver chain. His black hair looks silky and the smell of aftershave drifts into my nose. He grins and holds up two, beyond beautiful, red roses. I couldn't help but grin too as I take them out of his hands. I smell them close to my nose, my lips kissing so that I won't get cherry lip gloss on them.

"My mom thought you would like them," Dillon said, smiling shyly and peeking at his shoes.

"They're gorgeous," I smell them once more. "Thank you."

He stares at me, blinking like he didn't think I'd love them. Then he grins so large that his dimples look as deep as the Grand Canyon. I let out a giggle that makes him blush.

Dillon waits by the front door as I run into the kitchen and search for a vase. I find one under the sink and quickly fill it with cold water. I gently set the two roses inside and place it beside an opened window.

I step in front of the flat screen T.V. to get Jamui's attention. He barely blinks, like he can see right through me.

"I'm leaving," I inform him.

He ignores me.

I look at Saultan and Islamiat. I'm afraid to leave him here with Jamui. What happens if there's a fire and Jamui just sits on the couch ignoring life around him? What happens if there's a robber and he kidnaps Islamiat and kills Saultan? Anything could happen while I'm gone; Islamiat could even break a leg or Saultan accidentally cut himself badly.

I walk over to the kitchen table and sit in the seat next to my little sister. She's only in 8th grade and I don't want her to be responsible for everything that happens when I'm gone because Jamui's not capable. But…I still have to warn her. Nothing's happening to my only sister.

"Islamiat-"

"Don't worry, I have it all taken care of," she assures me. She smiles. "You look pretty. Just have a good time and grab a kiss at the end."

I give her a hug and a small kiss on Saultan's forehead. I give Jamui a rough goodbye.

When I get back to Dillon, he leads me outside and toward his red corvette. He helps me inside and starts the car up. We pass through the gate and I slowly breathe in and out.

Dillon is, sort of, rich. Like me. His mom and mine work in the same hospital as surgeons. Which gets you a lot of money. But I have more money than Dillon only because my father's a lawyer. Dillon's dad had a sickness that couldn't be treated. He died when Dillon was seven. But Dillon's mom makes enough money to make people believe there's a man in the house.

While Dillon's driving, I try to knock a retarded and disturbing eyelash out and away from my eye. It's difficult without using my hands or even a mirror. But after a while, I feel the eyelash fall, my eyeball free with its space.

I look at the unknown stores and restaurants we pass. I realize I've never been on this side of Hampton before. It looks richer.

"Where are we going Dillon?" I ask, kicking off my flats.

"It's a surprise," he tells me.

"You know I hate surprises."

He laughs. "You don't trust me?"

"Why would you think I wouldn't?"

He points his eyes at me.

"Of course I trust you," and I meant it.

We arrive at a fancy restaurant filled with people. Dillon parks between a silver Rolls Royce and a black Mercedes. I put my feet back in my flats, suddenly glad that I dressed this nice. (Darn, I should've worn the heels.) This is a restaurant you'd find famous people. I know Dillon has money for this place- his mom always gave him money. I'm sure he has five hundred bucks in his wallet right now.

I was about to open the car door to let myself out, when Dillon softly grabs my wrist and pulls me towards him. A quick second I think we're about to kiss. And I can't believe how much I want to. How I actually want to have those lips pressed against mine. And how I actually want to answers May's question and do what Islamiat said to.

Slowly, Dillon's hand grazes my cheek right below my eye. I blink and feel my lips push up just wanting to touch his. His lips are so close to mine. So close-

"Eyelash."

I look down at his hand, confused. Dillon is holding a skinny eyelash in front of my face. It's mine, the one that was giving me a hard time. And it had just ruined everything.

I back away fast. "Thanks," I say hard.

Dillon drops it in my hand. "Make a wish."

I close my eyes but it doesn't take long to think of what I want. After I'm done I blow it out of my palm.

Dillon helps me out the car. The chilly air covers my whole body, trying to get to my skin. He puts his arm around my shoulder which pulls me close to him and his leather jacket that smells like mints. It wasn't a boyfriend/girlfriend type of arm-over-the-shoulder, but a buddy one. But it's comforting which keeps me from moving away from him. Plus, it's cold.

Dillon holds the door open for me. I walk in, him right behind me. The scene takes my breath away.

The place is crowded. It's probably so crowded that it's a fire hazard. Waitresses and waiters shove through each other with food or drinks on their trays. It isn't one of those dead quiet restaurants where it seems the couples whisper to one another. It's loud and comfortable with everyone laughing and talking as loud as they wish. Nice, swaying music is playing from the speakers hanging on the walls. The bar is especially noisy where older guys and young couples drink and loudly chat. It reminds me of the cool kids at school when it's lunch time.

I look up at Dillon as he grabs my hand and leads me toward the hostess busily answering calls and scribbling down names. There are a bunch of people sitting on brown benches around the entrance waiting for a table, but Dillon walks through and around them, tugging me along with him.

Dillon releases my hand and waves it in front of the hostess's face to grab her attention. Once she looks directly up at him, she blinks once then twice.

"Dillon…Dillon Evans?" she asks, confused and surprised.

Dillon grins from ear to ear. "Miss me?"

She runs around her dark brown desk and jumps into Dillon's opened arms, bypassing me. She lets him go and holds his face in her hands.

"When your mom called for a reservation for two," she explains, "I didn't expect it to be for you and…" she finally notices me and smiles. "And a beautiful girl."

I blush and quickly look away.

"Alicia, this is Mariam," Dillon introduces me.

Shockingly, Alicia pulls me into her arms. Her hug is warm and loving, making me feel safe.

"Dillon has nice taste," she tells me.

Dillon's cheeks burn. "Um…"

"You know, when I used to take care of him when he was five, he'd tell me how he's going to date a beautiful girl," she giggles with a shake of her brown hair.

"Oh, Alicia," Dillon speaks, getting irritated.

"I guess he wasn't lying. Your guys seat is ready- go have a wonderful time," Alicia said, squeezing my arm like how grandmas do to a kid.

She turns around to face Dillon, back to being serious. "And *you* better take good care of her."

After promising, Dillon pulls me away from Alicia and to our table at the back of the restaurant. He pulls out my chair for me and waits for me to sit on the soft, red cushion before pushing it forward.

He sits across from me and rests his hands on the dark red tablecloth. He stares at me as I look through the menu.

"Uh, sorry about Alicia," he said, still staring.

"It's okay," I said. My mom would've taken him for my boyfriend too. "So, she used to babysit you?"

He shrugs, bringing his eyes off me and onto the menu. "Yeah. She's more like an aunt though."

"Seems like she loves you."

"That's what she says."

"So…have you brought Nelci here?" I question him.

He sighs like that's the worst thing I could ask. "I don't want to talk about her."

"Then what do you want to talk about?"

It seems like he hesitates. "Us."

I choke on the water I'm sipping. Dillon leans over the table to wipe the water off my chin with his napkin.

"You alright?"

"What about us?" I dismiss his question.

He leans back in his seat, staring at his hands resting on the table. "I know what I did, Mariam. There's no reason for you to forgive me. But I'm saying sorry and asking to start over."

I look at him, speechless.

"I never stopped thinking about you. You always made me feel good about myself. I miss you."

"But you never came back," I whisper to myself.

I knew he heard me when he looks up at my face.

"I wanted to, but I didn't believe you'd take me back."

"Why wouldn't I?" I ask him. "Dillon, you're my best friend. You're *always* my best friend," I add.

"Sometimes- when I think of you- I wish I was more," he mumbles.

I suck in my breath. My heart beats quicker. He wishes he was more? That's what I want, wasn't it? I mean, isn't it? I still want him to be more with me. Right? I feel scarily confused. More confused than I ever had.

I stand up as a short, smiley waitress walks up to our table, pencil and notepad in her hand.

"Hi, are you guys ready to order?"

I ignore her and point my words at Dillon. "Dillon, you're going out with Nelci and it would be a shame to destroy that. It's not that I don't like you. It's just you were always my best friend and changing so suddenly might be too weird for both of us."

"Mariam-" he says.

"I'm sorry, but this wasn't a good idea."

I push my purse back onto my shoulder and begin walking away from our table. I hear Dillon's chair screech as he gets up. I slip through the large crowds of people and tables as I try to get to the door before Dillon gets to me. I see it up ahead, in front of Alicia, the door swinging open and close as people trail in.

"Mariam!" Dillon shouts from behind me. I pretend not to hear him.

A cold hand snatches my arm. "Miss, someone's calling you.

I look down at the guy sitting in the booth with his hand grabbing my wrist, his long, black hair overlapping his eyes. His other big hand resting on the table. A black cloak hanging on him. His smile too familiar. Too creepy. Something I keep seeing in my dreams.

I scream.

CHAPTER 4

After my show in the restaurant, Dillon took me home. He even walked me up the stairs and into my room. I remember May asking him what was wrong with me and Ashley accusing him for drugging me. I was shaking so much I felt like barfing.

Dillon left and May and Ashley put me in bed. They threw the covers over my body and shut off the light. I couldn't help myself from falling asleep.

When I wake up a little after twelve, I already knew my best friends had gone home. But they left me a note, demanding me to call them and explain what happened. I throw it away.

I can barely explain to myself what happened. But I know what I saw. And I'm not denying it, ever. It was *him*. I'm sure of it. And now he's stalking me because…because…

I *know* what I saw!

But still, I pace around in my room asking myself if it was just maybe someone who talked like him and smiled like him. And wore the same cloak. Or maybe I just didn't feel good and was imagining things. Or maybe…

Maybe it really was him. Why try to deny it? No guy can talk and smile the same as another unless he has a twin. And I felt perfectly fine even before I walked into the restaurant. It's not like someone dropped some potion into the water that was served to me.

"It was him, Mariam," I tell myself. "No one but him."

My sister's murderer is haunting me.

Once I appeared downstairs, Islamiat crowded me with questions about my date last night. I didn't answer either one of them. Instead, I grabbed my license and stole Jamui's keys. I took his truck parked in the driveway also.

I needed time to think, so I head straight to the park. Kids are on the playground and parents sit on the benches, having conversations with neighbors. There's dogs being walked and they tug on their leashes and bark at blowing leaves. Even though there's a December breeze and some mornings you wake up and the grass is covered with ice, adults still believe in taking their afternoon walks and some kids have been running around on the playground for so long that their jackets have been taken off.

I drive past the park, having to step on the brakes before I slam into two boys who decided to sprint across the street at the last minute. After they get to the other side safely, I keep going. I drive away from the park as far as I can until the road stops. I climb out and drop the keys in my pocket. The freezing air touches my fingers and I wish I remembered to get gloves so I wouldn't have to cut off my fingers because of frostbite. I stuff them in the slots in my jacket and begin walking.

There's a wet and icy gate that ends the road and a sign that says 'DO NOT DRIVE PAST HERE', but there's no sign that's against walking. I bend down and under the gate. Up ahead there's a canopy of large, beautiful trees. It used to be where I and Dillon would go to just fool around and be the carefree kids we were. But that was a long, long time ago. This time the place has been introduced to May and Ashley and it's *our* place now.

The further I walk, the more the tall trees close in. The air gets warmer as I get crowded by trees. There's no path to follow, but I know this way by heart. I've been escaping here since I was eleven.

Soon, the trees begin to part. I turn left at the sign of the tree that's shaped like a little boy dancing. The farther I go, the more the grass looks greener, the trees appear newer, and the leaves seem fresher. I breathe in the air and I feel as if my problems recede, allowing me the pleasure to have no thoughts of trouble.

Then there's the sound of water and bugs. Flowers appear- a circle of yellow lilies and yellow tulips, pink roses by a tall Redbud tree, and white daisies growing beside the pond. The pond water flows down a small hill and disappears around a corner that's hidden by thorny bushes. The log is still there like it has been for years, right beside the water on a plate of green grass and small weeds.

I sit on the log. Some days I'd dip my feet in the water. Today, it'll probably freeze my blood to icicles. I'd rather not have that happen.

My phone buzzes in the back of my pocket. I'm not answering it, I think to myself. I have a strong feeling its May or Ashley. They'd know I'd be up by now and they're both wondering why I haven't called them yet. No way would it be my parents, they'd be too busy working.

I put my arms on my legs and put my face in my hands. I shut my eyes, breathing in and out like a normal person. I tell myself to relax and I just now realize how tired I still am.

I hear the flap of wings and watch a crow fly and steady its clawed feet on a tree branch. That's weird; I don't see those a lot around here, especially with this weather. Its eyes are paper white and the black in the middle looks like a nightmare. I stare at it as it checks me out.

Then suddenly the bird opens its beak and horrible words come out.

"You will never find me."

"You will never find me."

"You will never find me!"

I yelp and jump onto my feet as the crow gets louder.

"Go away!" I shout at it. It keeps screeching.

I pick up a rock and chuck it towards the bird. The crow beats its wings and lifts up into the air. The rock misses poorly but the crow gets the idea and disappears between trees. But it then circles around and lands a few feet away on the ground. Black smoke appears around it and the bird magically transforms into a man with large hands and dark hair and a black cloak. He smiles at me, a very sinister smile. I hold my breath.

The murderer picks up his feet and runs at me. I scream and fall on my butt like a pathetic little girl. I hold up my hands to protect myself but the murderer doesn't stop at me, but races past me. I turn around just in time to see him catch a little girl in his arms. She's looking at me with fear in her eyes, screaming and struggling in his arms. She parts her lips and asks a question with only seven words.

"Why did you let him take me?"

I open my eyes in a hurry. I get on my feet and check around me. There is no crow or murderer or little sister. I sigh. Just another stupid dream. Why did I let myself fall asleep?

Silence had token over except for the sound of falling water and low tweeting blue birds echoing around me. My phone rings on the floor. I pick it up and reject the call. I stuff my phone in my pocket and make a quick race to the car.

I need to get out of here.

I duck under the gate. I jog for the door handle and wrench it open. I know there is no crow and never was a crow, but I have a strong and certain feeling that staying here is not a good idea. I can sense him close. Watching. Observing. I can see his murderous smile in the back of my head. I can hear his cruel laughter tormenting my ears. I've never felt him so close before. That only shows that he's near and will do no good.

"Mariam!"

I jump high off my feet and might've screamed also if I hadn't covered my mouth with my hand. I press myself against the truck as two figures appear behind a blue convertible. I hold my breath, but then slowly start to calm down once I notice how feminine the two strangers are. A sigh of relief floods from my mouth the second I recognize the hopping, wavy hair.

"You don't answer my calls and now you jump when I say your name. I'm starting to wonder if you hate me," Ashley said.

They stop right in front of me. May has a silver scarf around her neck, her black coat buttoned up all the way with black, waterproof boots. Ashley has her hood up and her hands protected by soft, puffy gloves. You can tell she's wearing layers and her leather boots almost go to her knees.

May squeezes me with a hug. "I was so worried. I thought something bad had happened to you."

Ashley rolls her eyes and we share a smile. May will never stop being the worried mother.

"I'm fine," I assure her. "How did you guys find me?"

"You always come here when you're mad or worried," Ashley answers.

"Who said I'm mad or worried?"

"Well, you're here, aren't you?"

I shut my mouth. Ashley flashes her wicked smile at me. Fine, one point for her.

May lays her hand on my arm. "You want to talk about it?"

I become defensive. "There's nothing to talk about." There is no way I can tell them what I saw that night. *Who* I saw that night.

"Doesn't sound like it to me," Ashley mumbles.

I glare at her. She pretends not to notice and walks back to the blue convertible.

"I'm freezing," she calls back. "I'll wait inside the car with the heat up high while you ask her May."

Ashley climbs into the passenger side and shuts the door.

"Ask me what?"

"We're heading over to the mall," May said. "Will you *please* come?"

To the mall? A crowded, public place? Where it's easy to follow someone? Um, no.

"Thanks for the invitation, but…"

"I get it. You have no time for us," May said, bowing her head and pretending to cry.

"May, you know that's not it."

She sighs loudly. "What I know is that you don't like me."

I had to smile. "Fine, I'm coming."

"Yay!" she jumps up and down and pulls me to her car.

I get in the back. The car is already a nice warmth and my fingers are pleased they might not get frostbite after all. May starts the engine and I lay back and try to relax and act normal. And also try to pretend that I did not just have a dream about a crow appearing and speaking to me with exactly the same words with the same voice as that murderer.

"Mariam, are you okay?" Ashley asks, peering at me from the rearview mirror. "You look as if your about to barf."

I rub my forehead like that would scrub away my thoughts. "I'm all right."

"Hm," she goes, like she couldn't believe me any less. "So, how was last night?"

"Ashley!" May exclaims and shakes her head at her.

"What? You said you wouldn't talk about it. I never agreed to that."

"But she wants to keep her business to herself."

"Oh please! What's her business is our business. Don't be so easy, May," Ashley said.

"I'm not," May denies.

"Yes you are."

"Nu-uh."

Their voice, even though it's arguing, is as good as hot chocolate. It gives me something to listen to other than the warning the bad me is trying to yell through my mind. I lean back in my seat and actually begin to smile.

We get to the mall in ten minutes. Usually it takes fifteen-to-eighteen minutes, but not with May's driving. I think because her dad's a cop that it makes her think she's allowed to drive over the speed limit. I have no idea what made her believe that because if I was on the road along with May, I would seriously pull over and let her get far ahead. You know, just for safety measures.

We start right away, hitting the expensive stores first. I don't know how much money was on my credit cards. Enough to buy three pairs of jeans and six shirts, because that's exactly what I got. And that was only the first store.

We shop much more. May loves jewelry and Ashley loves shoes. Me, well, I love chocolate and nice shirts, so we definitely spent a while in See's Candy as I tried every sample they offered. After that, I left with two boxes of milk buttercream and one box of nuts and chews. May asked for some, but she saw the way I looked at her, like she was asking for my child, and decided she didn't want any anymore.

We enter more stores, trying on goofy glasses, heeled boots, and fancy hats. At one point a couple of boys came up to ask for our numbers. Ashley and I laughed in their faces while May giggled inside her mouth. I think they had no idea that we were about four years older than them.

The whole time with my friends really had me forgetting all the problems and mysteries stabbing at my life. Until we stop at May's favorite store.

"Oh, how pretty!" May calls out as soon as we walk into the store. The eight bags on her arms bounce and shake as she runs over to a gold dress. It's sleeveless and knee length. The gold has a glossy shine to it, the taffeta material crispy under and smooth on the surface.

May slips the dress off its hanger and brings it straight to *me*.

I put my hands up and the five bags on each arm slide to my elbows. "I don't think so, May."

"Come on. Please," she begged. "Just try it on."

"It's too small," I say.

"No excuses."

She pushes the dress into my arms and Ashley takes my shopping bags, grinning at me because I lost the war. I trump into the dressing room and the door clicks shut. I lock it and slip off my shoes. My shirt goes over and off my head and my jeans slide off my waist. I pull the dress on and my skin smiles at the beautiful fabric grabbing at my body. I walk up to the mirror stapled to the wall.

My excuse was actually true. The dress is too tight but I've never seen anything so beautiful. It literally glistens on me as I slowly turn in the mirror. Immediately, I think about how I could make this dress look better. With my hair up in a bun, my dark bare shoulders would be shown and it would look fascinating to have some glitter sprinkled on my skin. Light make up with maybe gold eye linear would bring out my eyes. And then my shoes could be…

I stop myself. I'm going too far too fast. Who said I was even buying it? I look at the price tag. Cheap for how much money I'm carrying on me, even with the double zeroes. But it's still too small.

"Mariam, how does it look?" May asks behind the door.

"Wonderful, but…it's too tight, May. I can hardly breathe," I explain.

"We'll find a larger size."

I hear her move away from the door and I sit down on a cushioned chair and wait.

In a few minutes there's a tap at the door.

"Bad luck girl," Ashley said. "There isn't a larger size. Actually, they said that's the only one they have left."

"Well I'm not going to lose ten pounds just to fit into it perfectly," I said. "I'm not getting it."

May whines. "But don't you want to wear it to junior prom."

"Who says I'm going to junior prom?"

"He might ask you," she said.

"Who's *he*, May?" I question her.

"You know- *him*," she whispers through the door.

The name Dillon floats through my head and I clench my fists. "No, I don't, May. So just drop it."

She groans and I begin peeling off the dress. I am sad not to get it. It's beautiful with its crispy taffeta material and golden shine. I've never seen a sleeveless dress like this or felt anything that clutches my body the way this does. If only it had my size, my number on the tag.

I reach for the hangar stuck on the hook and clipped to the wall. I gasp. Behind the hangar is another one with a dress dangling from its arms. A sleeveless dress with a gold gleam to it. *My* golden, sleeveless dress.

"That's impossible," I say under my breath.

But I guess not because it's hanging up right there before me. I take down the dress and fish for the tag. I stare down at the right number.

"May, we're both in luck," I tell her.

Ashley and May buy their few items they wanted to purchase. I find a darling pearl necklace. Everyone should have a pearl necklace, so I decided to buy it. I hand the dress and necklace to the elder, Chinese lady while my friends wait beside me.

The elder searches around the dress and that's when I realize that there isn't a price tag to find.

"Li-Hua!" the lady shouts for a young, Chinese woman sorting out a pile of pink high heels left on a bench. "Find me this dress with a price tag."

Li-Hua turns a corner and comes back a moment later. Right before she sets the dress on the counter, I notice something peeking out from under the dress.

"Look, there's the tag!" I exclaim.

"Oh!" the lady looks surprised to find it suddenly there now.

"Mom, your eyes are all wrong," Li-Hua said and laughs.

I pay for the dress and necklace and we hit two more stores before heading to the food court. I don't get much of anything in either store. All I want is some food before I pass out. Ashley and

May are finally done and I lead them into the line for hamburgers and fries.

I stuff myself with the food faster than May or Ashley ever could. I almost wanted more afterwards but knew I would regret it later if I swallowed anything else. I throw away the trash and wait at the table as my friends get up to get a cinnamon bun. Sitting there, I grab the bag with the golden dress, excited to see it just one more time. I lift it open and my heart practically stops.

It's not there. The bags empty except for the pearl necklace.

I drop it and open the other shopping bags of mine, scooting aside jeans and skirts. I search through eight of my twelve bags and the last four I literally toss everything out and onto the table, becoming more and more frantic by the second. I don't know if this is how a mom feels when they lose sight of their child, but if it is, it feels pretty darn horrible. I pull at my hair and chew on my lip.

My friends come over and Ashley's eyes are wide as she gawks at my shirts and designer jeans littered on the table.

"Mariam, what the hell?" she said.

"I can't find the dress," I admit.

"What!" May blurts.

I look up at them both. "Please tell me one of you put it in your bag for safekeeping."

They both shake their head.

"Great," I say and sit down, moaning.

"Okay, look, there's a rational explanation for this," Ashley said. "It's either in those last two stores or someone stole it."

"Someone stole it," I said right away.

"You don't know that," May said. "We should check."

"Good idea," Ashley agrees. "Mariam, you stay here while me and May check the last stores. You just keep searching through your bags."

"It's *not* here," I try.

"Just do as I say."

They disappear and I dig my hands through the shopping bags once again. When they come back, we each have no success.

I stand up abruptly and shove in my chair. "I'm getting my money back."

"That's not goanna happen," Ashley mutters. I ignore her and grab my shopping bags and make my way back to the store.

My friends follow behind me as I stomp into the store and find the counter. The same old lady is there and she seems not to notice my mood as I come to her.

"Problem?"

"Yes, there's a problem," I say. "My dress, the gold one- it's gone. Someone stole it."

She blinks at me. "What am I supposed to do about it?"

"I want my money back. I only had the dress for twenty minutes, maybe even less."

She reaches out her hand. "Let me see the receipt."

I rummage in my purse for the receipt. I pull it out; the edges bent and crinkled. I drop it in her hand.

"It should be on there," I said. She ignores me and inspects the receipt. She looks up at me for a second and then back down.

"Um," she scratches her chin, "all that's on here is a pearl necklace."

"That's not right," I say, confused. May and Ashley step up beside me.

"Maybe you didn't get the dress from here," she suggests.

"Maybe you should at least try to help out my friend, old lady," Ashley speaks up.

"Ashley, don't," I stop her. I turn my attention back to the woman. "There was someone else here. I think she was your daughter."

"Li-Hua?" she asks.

"Yes!" My hope rises.

"She left twelve minutes ago."

And then lands face-first into the ground like someone who couldn't open their parachute soon enough.

"No, no," I rub my head. "Look, I bought the dress here. I know I did."

“I’m sorry, but I’m getting old and I forget things.”

I stare at her. How the heck is that supposed to help me?

“Give me that.” I snatch the receipt from her hand and scan over it.

Though the paper is wrinkled and now there’s a large hole at the bottom, I can still make out the purchase I made. And pertaining to the receipt, I only made one purchase. Which is the pearl necklace, and *only* the pearl necklace. Something’s very wrong here.

I lean against the counter as a searing pain rushes through my head. I groan and drop the receipt. Ashley grabs my arm.

“You don’t look so good, girl,” she comments.

I hardly hear her, struggling to breathe as I ponder over the fact that I know I bought the dress. But even now it feels as if that thought is vanishing. The dress was gold and it had sleeves. Wait, no, it didn’t have sleeves. I think. Oh my God.

What’s happening to me?

CHAPTER 5

Monday morning, I wake up before my alarm does. I prepare myself for school, tying up my hair and eating a warm, blueberry muffin. I stand outside before the driver even appears.

At exactly ten-eleven at night, I forgot completely of the dress. I remember the accident about not having something I should, but of what, I have no clue. But I know something's missing and it hurts my head to think about it too much. So I ignore the feeling of a lost item. Even though when I open my closest I feel it, I pretend it's not there.

At lunch, May just *has* to bring up junior prom. Ashley's sitting beside me, eating the school's undercooked pizza. The sandwich the nanny kindly packed for me tastes dry, which is weird because her sandwiches are usually as good as ice cream. All I can do is stare at it, as if that will give it some flavor.

"We need to go shopping for a dress, girls," May said, even though junior prom isn't for four months. She blinks at her Caesar salad like she forgot the lettuce.

Something rings in my head. "Dress?" I mumble.

"You say something?" May asks.

"Didn't we already buy…a dress?"

Ashley looks at me sideways. "What on Earth are you talking about?"

Suddenly, a boxer's fist beats itself against my skull. My eyes fill up with tears from the pain and I moan loud.

May's expression turns from calm to worry in an instant. Ashley touches my shoulder.

"Mariam, do you need to go to the nurse?" questions Ashley.

"No, I'm fine." I look up at May and give her a reassuring smile but I have no idea if she even saw it on my face.

The bell rings and I jump out of my seat.

"See you guys later," I promise and move for my final three periods. But then I walk right into Dillon and his perfect girlfriend under his arm outside the lunch room.

"Dillon! What are you doing here?" I wonder, trying so hard not to rush with my words and praying my hair is where it's supposed to be.

He raises his eyebrows at me. "I go here."

Nelci smirks at me. I bet it would be much harder to smirk with a jacked up face. I can make that happen.

"Oh, right," I said, doing my best to ignore the chick.

"How are you feeling?" Dillon gives me a smile.

I don't return it, though later on I feel bad about it. "Much better."

Nelci sighs loudly and moves closer to Dillon's chest. "Are you goanna walk me to class or not?"

"Uh, yeah. Yeah, sure," Dillon says it as if he just remembered. His eyes twinkle as they watch my face. "I'll talk to you later, Mariam."

"Ok," I nod and his shoulder touches mine when he walks past me. Nelci throws me a glare, and this time, I give it right back.

The last period of the day finally comes. What sucks is that the day has to end with Mrs. Olden. The best person you want if you need your day ruined. At least I didn't walk in late like the other kid did. He has detention now.

When the day ends, Mrs. Olden passes back the tests we took Friday. I get myself ready for my either horrible or decent grade, because there is no way I got a perfect score. But when Mrs. Olden gets to my desk, she doesn't drop a test on my desk with her lips pursed. Instead, she bends down and whispers in my ear, "See me after class." She then walks away, leaving me confused and stuck listening to the other students brag and whine about the grade they got.

The bell rings and everyone except me and the teacher jumps out of their seats and runs out the door before Mrs. Olden assigns homework.

A blanket of silence hoods over the classroom. I get up and walk to her desk. She pays attention to the papers scattered in her view. I clear my throat and she looks up at me.

"You wanted to talk to me," I remind.

"Right," she says.

She opens a drawer to her left and takes out a piece of paper. I step closer and realize it's the test we took on Friday, but blank.

"Tell me why you turned this in on Friday," she said.

"That's not mine," I clarify.

"This *is* yours. You turned this in."

I stare at the blank test as my hands begin to tremble.

Mrs. Olden lays her hand on the test, her nails sharp and green. "Listen, Mariam. I know I'm hard on you and that's because you're an athlete. You need to do good to play sports. And this," she taps the test, "is unacceptable. You're so much better than this-"

"No, Mrs. Olden, you don't understand," I speak up. "I took the test. I did. At first I couldn't because um…"

My voice trails off. Damn it, what was it? Something's missing.

The teacher sighs. "At least I know you weren't purposely trying to get on my nerves. You didn't even put your name on it. But this is going as a zero in the grade book. You could've tried at least one problem."

My eyes light up. A zero is worse than an F. "Let me retake it."

"I can't do that. I'm very sorry but you're failing my class now."

"But volleyball tryouts-"

"I said I'm sorry."

She turns her attention off of me and my hands still shake and tears burn behind me eyes.

I grab my test and rip it in half in front of her face. She purses her lips and begins to say something but the door slamming cuts off her words.

I make it outside without a teardrop. And then I suck it up so no one will notice my watery eyes. Ashley and May aren't in sight. Good for that because listening to someone else's voice right now will perhaps have me punching an innocent tree. I see Nelci by the bushes with her crew and I get the fantasy of breaking her nose and shredding her oh-so-perfect hair. She sees me looking and sneers. She whispers something in the blonde's ear and they both start giggling. I almost chuckle. Don't tell me she wants to be at the end of my fist.

"Stupid girl," I murmur, but keep moving.

"Miss Wilson."

I stop in my tracks. I know that voice.

"Do you have a minute?"

I definitely know that voice. I look behind my shoulder. There she stands, at the end of the steps, with a rain coat over a white blouse and black jeans tight around her thin legs. My worst nightmare.

I stand like a statue as she walks up to me. Delicately traced eyeliner darkens the space around her green and blue eyes. Her hair is up in a teenage bun, which shouldn't look good on an adult, but does on her. Maybe because her skin still looks young and she smiles as if she's going to a party after the football game.

"Is there something you need, Agent Clark?" I ask.

"Please, call me Shelly," she said.

"And you can keep calling me Miss Wilson," I tell her, my shoulders stiff.

She clenches her jaw a little and it's like some of her beauty flies away. Then she releases the pressure and her beauty rests at a spot.

"Five minutes. That's all I'm asking. I can take you home," she offers.

"Thanks, but I have a driver who's probably tired of waiting for me," I said, turning on my heels.

"I sent him home."

I turn back around, my eyes on fire. "You did what now?"

"I convinced him to take the day off."

"That's just perfect," I groan.

"And you can walk home," she recommends, "though have fun with that. But I'll be at your house waiting for you."

I stare at her for a while. The fact that she's bothering me again must mean that it's something important. Only, the problem with Agent Clark is that whatever comes out of her mouth is never good and never helps me out. I mean, she *is* the woman that made my fear list bigger and has me sleeping with horrible nightmares that won't go away no matter how hard I or Ms. Bell tries. But if I say no, she'll never leave.

"Five minutes," I said. "I'll give you that much and then you take me home."

"Sure," she says.

That doesn't sound very convincing, but I have no ride and walking home is something I'd rather not do with this weather.

"Lead the way," I order.

I follow Agent Clark to the parking lot. There's a guy leaning against his truck, talking into his cellphone with a scowl. Three girls giggle in an old corvette, their hair blonde and their outfits flimsy. A boy with his belt hardly holding up his jeans and his glasses edging off his nose, runs after a red head that has his keys in her thieving hands. I sidestep away from them as they stop next to me and he snatches the keys out of her fingers.

Agent Clark halts at a yellow beetle and takes out her car keys. There's a beep and she opens the driver's side.

“You’re kidding,” I said.

“What’s the problem?” she asks, confused.

“Uh, nothing,” I say and get in the front with her.

Driving out of the parking lot, she makes a left instead of a right. The wrong turn.

“Um, we are going to my house, right?” I ask. Don’t play any games with me Shelly.

“Yes, this is just a simpler route,” she explains. “Less traffic.”

But does it get me home in five minutes?

“Talk,” I tell her.

She sighs like this is going to be the hardest thing she’s ever done.

“This is going to be a little difficult…for the both of us,” she begins.

“Why?”

“It’s about your sister, Miss Wilson. The one that passed away.”

I don’t want to talk about this. I don’t want to talk about this. I keep saying it over and over in my head.

“I’m sure you don’t want to talk about this,” Shelly says. So nice that she can read my mind. “But it’s very important and someone must know. Especially you.”

Just spit it out, I want to say, but I keep staring out the window at all the other vehicles, wishing I was in either one of them except this one.

“Shelly,” I interrupt the intense moment, “on Friday, how did you know I was sick?”

She seems not to expect that question. “Your mom told me.”

“But how would you know I could die?”

She doesn’t speak quickly enough to make me believe her response is going to be good. “When you use your gift wrong, it will treat you no better.”

“I don’t have a gift,” I tell her.

"Well, whatever you want to call it, it will literally try to destroy you from the inside. What happened Friday was just a demo. What happens later might end your life."

"*What* might end my life?" I beg her for the answer.

"Your gift," she says.

"I told you, I'm not gifted."

"Then you must not be the girl who had her little sister murdered," she raises her voice. "On the streets. Board daylight, screaming her head off, but *no one* came to help. That's what you told the cops. No one came. But I'm here now. I know I wasn't there *then*, but I'm here *now*. I'm here to help you find him."

My hand goes to my forehead. "I don't want to talk about him."

Shelly takes a left and I know for sure we're going the wrong way. "And why not?"

I puff out a sigh. I need to tell *someone* what happened and how I'm feeling. "I saw him."

"Where?" she asks, very interested.

"At a restaurant on the other side of Hamptons. He was inside the same restaurant that I was in. He *touched* me. What does he want?"

"I should've come quicker," she grumbles.

"What's going on?" I demand.

Shelly breathes slowly. "Miss Wilson, do you remember how your sister was killed?"

I shudder. A vision of her head cut open comes to mind. "How could I forget?"

"You had a huge gash in the back of your head that caused you brain damage. You blacked out before she died. When the murderer killed her by hitting her in the head with his," Shelly takes a shaky breath like she doesn't even want to remember how a little girl like her died- "with his axe, it left a hole in her head also."

A hole a lot bigger than mine was, I thought.

"In her few last precious seconds left to live, something supernatural happened," Shelly said, looking at me sideways.

"Which was what?" I asked.

The agent sighs very slowly. "Miss Wilson, your sister had the ability to create anything that came to mind whether it was a pencil or a car. It was passed on to you."

"My sister was not gifted," I tell her, forcefully. My dream keeps running up into my brain, making me think too much. It was just a dream. It's impossible to do something like that in real life. "She was only three," I add, like that would help.

"Age has nothing to do with it."

"I don't have some special superpower," I said, my voice rising.

"Really?" she wonders. "Then how do you explain that test you got back today that you *know* you took. And don't forget the dress you bought yesterday. Where is it now? Or did you already forget about it?"

"So there was a dress," I said. It feels so good to have the right information back in my head.

"Oh, there was a dress. But your head probably hurts whenever you think about it, huh?"

"You've been stalking me," I state.

"No, I've been protecting you," she corrects.

"From who?"

"I think we both know who the big problem is."

She looks at me and it's almost like I can see his face in her eyes.

"Tell me what he wants," I said, struggling to stay calm and not burst out curse words about him.

Shelly tightens her lips. "That information is confidential unless I know I have your trust."

My trust?

Trust is a big thing for me because you never know when someone is just going to let you drown in the water. To some people, trust is a fantasy and to others, it's a way for saying I love you. I trust Dillon and my parents. Ashley and May occasionally. Jamui, not so much. But Shelly? Everything she made me tell her three months ago still haunts my dreams.

But he's out there. I saw him with my own eyes. We made contact. And he wants more than just to see how I'm doing.

"I trust you," I spit out.

She swerves to the right, jumping onto the freeway and forgetting my house entirely.

"His name is Ike Henderson," Shelly tells me, slapping a black and white photo of him on her desk.

Shelly's office is the size of a regular family room. A brown desk with a black chair behind it. Two plain chairs sitting in front, with me in one. And then other stuff you'd expect in an office: computer, lamp, bookshelf, files, and papers staked on her desk. Her walls are dark red with pictures clinging to the side of the two windows, and a big wooden fan over my head.

I stand up and lean over the desk to get a closer look of the picture. It's a mug shot. It's the murderer, but younger with crazy hair that had to be orange or red.

Shelly clarifies, "Ike got into trouble with drugs when he was seventeen. His father was an abusive alcoholic. Died about four years ago. His mom was shot when he was eleven."

Hard life, I thought. Still gives you no right to end other lives.

"What's up with him now?" I ask, suspicious.

"Well, he used to live in Georgia, and then moved out of the country. That was two-in-a-half years ago, when he was twenty. He now moves from place to place, not exactly having a house," Shelly explains. "And…he works alone."

I look up. "Doing what?"

"Killing young children."

My eyelids shut and I clench my fists. My sister's screams echoes through my head and I see the murderer's face, Ike, sneer at me, his hand flying through the air to meet my cheek.

You will never find me.

I shudder at the words. Shelly notices but doesn't consider to ask a question.

"Once he got back in the country," she starts, "we noticed children under the age thirteen being murdered. Rapidly. Every two weeks."

"Well, how do you know he did all of them?" I asked.

"There was something different about their blood. Something special," she says. "And, he told us."

"He *told* you?" I repeat confused.

"His first murder was a young girl. Eight years old. Stabbed in the back multiple times in her bedroom." I don't make a sound, so she keeps going. "I investigated the crime scene with my other partners. Taped to the wall for everyone to see was a note that said, 'there will be more'."

"That's it?" I ask.

She shrugs. "That's it. But he left the pen. We took his prints and got our guy."

I nod. "He wanted you to find the pen."

"He sure did. He's been at it for more than two years now."

Killing kids every two weeks for two years?

"How come this doesn't get on the news?" I wonder.

"Parents would freak out if they knew a serial killer is out there murdering innocent kids. Sometimes it does get out, twice or three times, but we just make sure that we're more careful next time. The media doesn't need to know about this, it would do more harm than good."

I keep silence. I was one that got on the news. Everyone knows about me. Everyone.

Shelly continues. "He's hard to catch- never staying at a place more than one day. He changes his looks all the time. What did he look like this time?"

"He had black hair covering his eyes," I answer.

Shelly nods like she knew all along. "Yes, he's changed recently. The first time you seen him, you said he had curly, brown hair."

I back away from the table. I wrap my arms around myself and stare at the floor. I slowly sigh.

"Why d-does he do it?" I stutter.

"That's where things get tricky," she answers.

Agent Clark touches her ear and I realize there's an earpiece.

"Dr. Jeff, are you ready for us?" she speaks into it.

I don't hear the response, but she holds down the shift button on her computer and presses keys Z and C at the same time. There's a click and a snap and the bookshelves behind Shelly's desk break apart as a steel door appears.

"Follow me," she directs, taking out a key and unlocking the door.

At first I forget how to move. Finding out there's a door hiding behind a bunch of books is a little surprising. I walk around the desk and step inside the secret room behind Shelly. The door shuts behind me.

The room is bright and filled with alien machines beeping and churning. The loud noise irritates my ears some, but I try my best to ignore it. The floor is white tile and it makes my shoes squeak. The room is freezing and smells of medicine and smoke and animals. I cross my arms and move closer to Shelly.

A man appears before me. He's a short, tanned man with a brown mustache matching his brown, shaggy hair. His eyes are crystal blue and would look a lot better on a model. He's wearing a lab coat with black sneakers. He has the same earpiece in his ear that Mrs. Clark does.

"Miss Wilson, this is Dr. Jeff," Shelly introduces.

We shake hands and Dr. Jeff gives mine a pat before letting go. He smiles bright.

"It's an honor to meet you, dear," he says. There's sweat on his forehead and his hands aren't dry either, but his eyes and smile are kind and hopeful.

"Really?" I said. "How come?"

"Well, you're one of many that hold the gift of creating objects from your own mind. Tell me, what have you made so far?"

I look at Shelly. She nods at me.

"I don't really remember. I think a dress is one of them," I answer. I shrug.

Dr. Jeff chuckles. "I see you're a beginner. It's okay, anybody is better than nobody."

I didn't know how I was supposed to react to that, but soon he was moving forward and I had to follow. Shelly's beside me and I give her the question I'm starting to think: what am I doing here?

"Dr. Jeff knows anything and everything about your gift," she said.

"The gift I'm pretty sure I don't have?" I ask.

"No, the gift I'm pretty sure you do have."

Prove it, I want to say, but then she'd just bring up my blank test and dress that vanished. It's not enough for me.

We walk along with Dr. Jeff through the huge, white lab. There are people with white coats standing by each machine. A tall gray one lets out a buzzing noise and a tray slides out of a slot on the machine with a cylinder tube standing up in the middle. A man grabs the tube and sniffs the green liquid inside the cylinder. He nods in approval and brings it to a lab table to inspect further. Another machine beeps loud and two people move to work on it while a third machine to my right seems to be churning like a wash machine. I notice fans twirling over my head, fans twice their normal size. The sound of tiny feet scrambling around a cage grabs my attention. I look to my left, able to see a hamster make its way up a staircase to eat some weird looking purple food. A white rabbit hops to the corner of its cage, its red eyes gazing at me. There are a few more cages of trapped animals as we keep walking on. Mice, frogs, and even a lone monkey in a large cage.

We end up all the way at the back of the laboratory. There are no animals or loud, annoying machines. Only a desk with a microscope and computer, an exam table, and a tall scanner. There's a tray on the desk with medical scissors and knifes, but Dr. Jeff ignores those as he sits in his chair with wheels.

He grabs thin glasses out of his drawer and sets them on his nose. He motions me to him and I step closer.

He takes my left hand and inspects it close to his face. He does the same with my right. He peers into my eyes with a flashlight and I open my mouth wide when he tells me to, searching for something that's not visible. When he's through, he sets down the flashlight and puts away his glasses.

"Doesn't look like anything's wrong,' he said. "What happened Friday didn't cause any lasting damage."

"What were you looking for?" I ask, curious.

"Purple under the skin in your hands that look like nasty bruises or blood in your eyes. If your throat and tongue seems to look as if it's turning black and scratchy is a sure sign that whatever you did, your gift *did not* like," he explains.

My gift. I sigh and lean against the exam table.

"Have you had any trouble breathing? Has your eyesight seemed to get worse?" Dr. Jeff questions.

I shake my head.

"Then your fine dear. No need to worry."

"That's not why I'm worried. You guys think I'm something I'm not. I have *no* gift."

Shelly and Dr. Jeff both look at each other. Shelly gives a quick nod that's hardly noticed. I notice a lot of things that I shouldn't.

"I don't have proof to prove to you that your special, Mariam," said Dr. Jeff. "But I do have facts."

He moves us to the computer at his desk. He types at the keyboard and a PowerPoint pops up. The PowerPoint shows the letters and numbers X1 and X2.

"X1 is your sister and you are X2," he clarifies. He clicks the next slide.

It shows X2 with red in the background.

"X2- you Mariam- has just been knocked unconscious. The red indicates blood, meaning your bleeding from the large hole in your head."

He goes on to the next slide. X2 is still bleeding, but this time, X1 is bleeding too. My mouth goes dry. I have a feeling I know what this slide is trying to tell.

Dr. Jeff bows his head. "X1 has just been killed. The murderer brought his axe straight into her head. The axe made a massive hole and she died instantly. And that's when the magic happened."

The third slide shows bubble-like things trickling from X1 and heading to X2.

"The ones who carry the gift- I call them Constituters. It means to form or compose. The power is basically alive. It sleeps in the brain.

"When your sister died, it had to leave because it couldn't grow in a dying body," the doctor explains. "It had to find a different body. But the only way for it to enter a body is through the head to rest in the brain."

"And I was the closest one," I finish. "My head was open and I wasn't dead yet."

Dr. Jeff shrugs like you couldn't blame it. "It enters the closest body it can before it dies in the open air. It's like a cellphone. Your sister's death sent out the message and you received it."

"What I received is trying to kill me," I raise my voice.

Dr. Jeff gets off his seat. "No, my dear. It's not trying to kill you. If you die, it has to find a new home. The way you used it Friday made it irritated. If you kick a cat multiple times, it's going to scratch back."

"I'd rather have been kicked by a cat than what that thing did to me," I say.

"I'm sure you do. But when you learn how to master it, you'll be in control of it. Because right now, it controls you."

I turn around to face Shelly who's been so quiet the whole time. "How long did you know?"

"That you're a Constituter?" she asks. "A week ago, thanks to Dr. Jeff. He discovered that you're holding the uncommon blood that your sister used to hold, the blood that made her special. That

Ike Henderson murdered your sister? The moment you told me that you got hit by a car. A car that no one was driving. Ike is a Constituter just like your sister was. Just like you are."

"So what? He thinks that gives him the right to start murdering innocent kids?" I asked.

"I guess so. He hasn't stopped ever since he started. But that's not all."

"There's more?"

Shelly licks her lips. "He only kills Constituters. That's why your sister died, Miss Wilson. The selfish bastard won't let anyone but himself have the gift. He doesn't like to share."

That's why she died? Because she was special. I feel all the emotions spread through my body. Sad, lonely, hate. Revenge. Revenge lasts the longest.

"He seems to always get them before they pass the age thirteen," Mrs. Clark said.

"I'm seventeen," I mutter, mostly to myself.

The agent smiles. "Yes, and that's why we desperately need your help. I'm not certain if Ike knows if you're a Constituter, but he's suspicious or else he wouldn't be following you around. The plan is to give you control over your gift and stop Ike before he stops you."

That mostly ends with one of us dying, I think to myself. Then I remember my sister's funeral. My mom's tears falling down her cheeks, Dad's hands clenched at his sides. Jamui doesn't speak anymore and I can hardly look at a kid on the playground without thinking about her. Maybe that's how it's supposed to finish. Maybe one of use should die at the end.

It better not end up being me.

I look at the agent. "I don't- I can't – die. Do you know what will happen if my parents lose another girl. Jamui will kill himself if he knows I'm dead. My little brother and sister won't believe in anything else. I can't die, Shelly," I say, beginning to tremble. Tears peak at the edges of my eyes and I swallow to keep them back.

Shelly comes up to me and grabs my hands.

"And you won't if you trust me. I am not going to let any more pain happen to your family. Okay?"

Her eyes are sincere and real and something inside me softens. I pull my hands from hers and slowly start to nod. "Okay, okay. What am I supposed to do?"

"Nothing now except learn," Shelly said.

"Learn?"

"The only way to have control over your power is to learn how to use it the right way," Dr. Jeff said.

"Exactly," Shelly agrees.

Alright, I guess that makes sense. But they're getting everything they need out of me. It's my turn to get something out of them.

"I want to make a deal," I speak up.

Shelly looks me over first as if trying to find a scheme hiding on my body. "Sounds fair."

"My therapist- Ms. Bell- I want you to end the meetings with me and her."

Shelly and Dr. Jeff look at each other. There's confusion on the doctors face and it seems like he's about to shake his head before the agent opens her mouth.

"It's a deal. It's not like what she was doing was helping anyways," Mrs. Clark said. "Ms. Bell is done being your therapist."

I sigh with relief. It feels good to get that lady permanently away from me. Making excuses every Thursday and pretending to not care about the words streaming out of her mouth is rough enough.

"Now, Miss Wilson, who's side are you on?" Shelly asks.

"Yours," I answer automatically.

She nods. "Good," she crosses her arms. "Someone will be at your door tomorrow after school. Good luck."

CHAPTER 6

"Mariam!" Ashley shouts.

I look at her. "What?"

"Did you hear anything I just said?"

"Um…" I think hard, "about volleyball?"

"Not only that," she says, rolling her eyes. "Try outs are Thursday and May's surprise *birthday* party."

My heart sinks when Ashley mentions volleyball. There's still an F in Mrs. Olden's class that I have yet to change. Thursdays in two days and there's no way to bring up my grade by then. I stab my salad with my plastic fork.

Then there's May's birthday. Ashley and I planned weeks ago to throw a surprise party. It's my job to set it up and make sure the food and drinks are there. Ashley's supposed to keep May away from her house until six. Her part is easy since May will go along with just about anything.

Ashley's still staring at me, waiting for my excuse.

"I'm sorry I just have a lot going on," I said.

"Oh, you mean about Dillon!" May hollers, scooting in next to me on the lunch table with her tray of food.

My eyes pierce at her for being so loud and she mutters a sorry. I peak at Dillon across the room. He's talking with his friends. I notice how Nelci would try to put her leg over his and he would move slightly away. What's his problem?

"You never said- did he ever kiss you?" May wonders.

"Uh," is all I say.

The bell rings at the perfect time. I grab my backpack off the floor and pull it over my shoulder. I tell my friends I'll explain everything later. I don't wait for their response as I scurry off to 5th period.

I didn't exactly understand the words coming out of my teacher's mouth, because I didn't bother listening. I knew there was a lot. But whatever it was, it must not of been too important because neither did anyone else. I worked on finishing my English and art homework before school ends. It wasn't easy; I had to guess on all of it. But at least I got it finished. When class ends, the teacher leaves us with no homework.

My last class, Algebra 2, felt like it was way more than fifty-five minutes. Mrs. Olden dragged us into groups, so I had to participate. I was afraid of thinking about things. What happens if I think and it…appears? That's sure to freak some of my classmates out.

I race out the classroom the minute the bell rings. I pray that Ashley or May won't be waiting for me by the front of the school like they do occasionally. I want to get home as soon as possible to prepare myself for whoever will come knocking at my door.

But the moment I step outside and hurry down the steps, it's not my friends that step in front of my path, but Dillon.

"Hey," he smiles.

"Oh, hi," I greet. My hand immediately goes to my hair and I slap it away mentally.

"Is there somewhere you need to be?" he asks.

"Sort of. Kind of. I'm expecting someone at home."

Dillon's hazel eyes stare at my face while I speak, as if wanting to catch every detail. Little flecks of sea green dance around his pupil and I almost smile.

"Expecting someone?" he says, almost to himself.

"Yes. A woman," I add, too quickly and too loud. I don't even know if it will be a boy or a girl at my door. Shelly didn't even give me a name. "She's supposed to be there right after school. I should go."

He grabs my hand and pulls me back to him. "Let me drive you home."

I try to stop my heart from beating as hard as I keep my voice as calm as possible so he won't know I'm freaking out inside.

"I have a driver who does that," I tell him, "but thanks."

He releases my hand to scratch his forehead, wearing the mask of guilt. "Uh, yeah. Actually, I told him to take the day off."

My mouth falls, shocked. I bend my head back as I say, "Okay, people really need to stop doing that."

There's a hint of a smile on Dillon's lips. Not that I'm watching his lips and thinking about them. I just happened to notice the smile while *glancing* over them.

Dillon takes my hand once again. "I thought you'd rather ride with your best friend in his *corvette*."

"That does sound tempting," I say.

Dillon's eyes shine. "There are leather seats and a new stereo too."

Rain hits my nose and slides down my jacket as it begins to sprinkle. I shiver from the cold.

"Did I also forget to mention that there's a heater?" he includes.

"Fine, you win," I surrender.

I feel giddy as he guides me to his vehicle in the parking lot. I think about watching out for Nelci but forget it. Why ruin this moment with her ugly face?

In the car, Dillon turns on the heater and heads to my house, leaning back with one hand on the wheel. I watch him as he drives. He looks my way, our eyes meet, and I look away first.

The guard sees me in the passenger seat and the gate unlatches and slides apart. The corvette drives through and stops in front of my house.

I take off my seatbelt and grab hold of my backpack. Dillon turns his body to me.

"I have something for you."

He reaches into the backseat and brings out a present wrapped in green paper. He puts it in my lap. Curious, I tear at the paper on the edges, forgetting my suspicious visitor and throwing all my attention on my surprising gift.

Under the wrapping paper is a shoe box. I flip the lid open and pull away the tissue paper.

Smiling back at me is a Barbie doll with brown curly hair spread out everywhere. A green take-top and blue jeans cover her body. Black high heels hang from her feet. I smile.

It's Madison.

"I thought of you yesterday and decided to find her for you," he explains.

I lean over and kiss him on the cheek before I could stop myself. "Thank you. I missed her."

He grins. "No problem."

I leave Dillon's car and walk up the stairs to my room. I'm clutching Madison so tightly, I'm afraid her head will pop off. I drop my backpack on my floor and rest Madison on my dresser.

The doorbell rings.

I race out of my room. The nanny's walking towards the door and I lean over the railing.

"Don't answer!" I shout down. "I will."

The nanny leaves it to me and I rush down the stairs. I stop in front of the door and slowly release my breath just like Ms. Bell says to do.

I unlock the door and open it to reveal the visitor and-

Speak. Of. The. Devil.

She grins and nods. "Good afternoon."

It *was* a good afternoon.

Ms. Bell pushes past me and surveys her surroundings.

"Um," I slam the door shut, "what are you doing here? I thought we won't be seeing each other anymore."

I was *really* hoping we won't be seeing each other anymore.

Ms. Bell touches the roses on the table. "I'm not here as your therapist."

"Then why are you here?" I ask. "I'm expecting a visitor."

"Mariam," Ms. Bell faces me, clasping her hands together, "I *am* your visitor."

"Ha-ha, that's hilarious."

But Ms. Bell's not laughing.

Oh no.

"Shelly, this is *so* not funny!" I yell into the phone.

"I agree," she says, sounding calm and collected. "I'm not trying to be funny."

"*What* is she doing here? We had a deal."

"And the deals still sealed."

"No, you broke it. We agreed that I and she won't be working together anymore."

I eye Ms. Bell leaning against the table with her eyes wondering around the place. We brought the commotion into the abandon library on the second floor and shut the door to not be bothered. She seems to soak in everything she sets her eyes on. It's irritating.

"Your wrong, Miss Wilson," Shelly said, her voice strict. "We agreed to end the meetings with you and her as your *therapist*. She's not there to help you with your social life. She's there as your tutor."

Ms. Bell's staring my way, unblinking. I lick my lips and turn my back on her.

"I don't like this," I complain.

"I wished you good luck," Shelly reminds. "How much do you need?"

I sigh into the phone.

"Remember who this is for, Miss Wilson."

The agent hangs up and I'm left listening to nothing but a buzz.

Ms. Bell loudly claps her hands together. “Well, I couldn’t ask for better hospitality than that.”

I set my phone on the table and face my therapist…or my *old* therapist. Her black heels click on the floor as she walks in a circle, peering at the tall shelves that hold books full of information no longer needed. This room just takes up space and collects dust. But still, it’s somehow Dad’s favorite room in the whole house.

“How much do you guys read?” she wonders.

I snort. “We don’t.”

I walk up to her, eye to eye. Ms. Bell patted on some blush and etched on eyeliner. Her lips are blue and dry from the cold and strands of her black hair have escaped from her ponytail.

Ms. Bell steps closer to me and I can smell lime wafting off of her skin.

“I knew you were special,” she whispers.

At least someone thinks so.

“Let’s begin, shall we?” she suggests, way too excited.

Ms. Bell complains about how little room this library offers. So together, we push the round tables and chairs and couches to one side of the wall, leaving much more room. She looks around and nods with approval at all the space we created. We left only one round table and two chairs in the middle of the room.

I sit in one of the chairs and watch Ms. Bell pull some papers out of her bag and scan over them.

“What’s that?” I demand.

“Just some info about you,” she answers, not bothering to look up.

I rise a little in my seat to see if I can catch some words on the papers. “Like what?”

“Your gift, that’s all.”

I bite my lip, desperately wanting to know what Shelly or Dr. Jeff decided to write down that Ms. Bell doesn’t look too eager to share with me.

Ms. Bell puts the papers back in the bag. She lays her hands on the table.

"Your problem is that you create but don't remember," she tells me, matter-of-fact.

"I do remember," I object.

"Really? What did you form to take the math test?"

I have no clue. "Forget that. I almost died that day. I would very much like that *not* to happen again."

"Yes, well, we can fix that while fixing the first problem. Stand up and open your right hand."

I do as she says and she grabs my wrist and raises my arm more to chin height.

"I want to see an apple," she orders.

"But I don't-" I begin

"Just do the best you can."

I do what she taught me to: breathe slowly. I shut my eyes and hold a picture of a perfect, green apple in my head. Not so hard. I feel something drop in my hand and I open my eyes.

I can hardly believe what I see. An apple, full and green, sits in my hand like I grabbed it off the table just now. I look at Ms. Bell to make sure she sees it too. She's grinning at me.

Then the apple turns droopy and completely transforms into warm liquid. It slides down between my fingers and over the edge of my palm. It falls towards the floor but right before it hits the ground, a bright light appears and sucks up the apple whole.

Ms. Bell's smile vanishes and my arms still up like I'm waiting for the apple to come back.

"Uh, was that supposed to happen?" I ask, unsure.

A buzzing begins in my head.

"Try again," Ms. Bell orders.

I listen to her demand but the apple turns out to be the same as the last one.

The buzzing in my head gets incredibly loud and I grab my head and moan. My hands and legs begin to shake as I feel bile rise in my throat. I swallow it back down with a struggle.

"I don't want to do this anymore," I groan. I sit down and try to force my nerves calm but I feel as Saultan does after he drinks three cans of soda: unable to stop moving.

Ms. Bell's in front of me. "Mariam, remember who's in control. The more you stop once it sends out pain, the stronger it gets. *You* are in control. You know exactly what you want. Make it *exactly* that way."

I put my hands down and lean back in my chair. My head stings and Ms. Bell's all in my face.

"Try again. And this time, really visualize the color. Remember the touch. Catch the scent. Recall the taste. Hold that all in your mind and never let go."

I shut my eyes tightly.

Green apple. It's hard and smooth. On the middle of the top is a brownish leaf growing out of it. The inside is creamy white with dark red seeds hidden in it. The taste is sweet, then sour, and sweet at the end. The smell is delicious and draws you towards itself. And the sound of when you bite into it, squishy and soft with a bit of a crunch.

I watch it blink into life in my own palm. My lips curve into a smile. I hold onto my thought as tight as a belt around a fat man's waist. The apple doesn't melt and the buzzing in my head fades away.

Ms. Bell bends on her knees to my height. "How do you feel?"

Without the irritating buzzing, the need to throw up, and knowing I have this apple on lockdown? Brilliant.

"I feel great," I speak truthfully.

"Very good," she stands up straight. "Now take it away."

I take my mind off the apple. It disappears, a bright light taking it someplace else.

The buzzing comes back, not as rough, but it's back.

There's no smile on Ms. Bell's face. "Bring the apple back."

I rethink the apple. The green look, the sweet smell and taste, the strong touch, and the squishy sound of when you bite into it. It comes into my hands in seconds. I love at how easy this is getting.

"And put it away," she says.

Confused, I let my mind go and the apple disappears with the light. My headache grows bigger and I bite my tongue so to not moan.

Ms. Bell sighs, shakes her head, and stares at me. "You're not doing it right. Give me back the apple," she commands.

"What? I don't what to, my heads beginning to hurt again," I said, frustrated. Don't scream, I think. Remember, this is for the kids. This is for my sister.

"I know. Make the apple."

I make an irritated grunt but think of the scent, smell, taste, and look of that stupid apple. It appears in my hand.

"Now," Ms. Bell said, talking slowly like I'm a dumb child, "put it away. But, I don't want to see a light this time."

"Why?" I question with some attitude.

"Because that's exactly why you're heads hurting. The light is *not* good."

I stare at her strangely. "How do you know this?"

Ms. Bell looks down at her hands. "I had a nephew with the same power as you. I was the only person that knew about his special gift. He told me everything about it and how to use it right. That's why Agent Clark assigned me to you."

"What happened to him?"

She clears her throat. This time, her voice cracks. "He was murdered when he was twelve. Last year."

"By…*him*?"

She nods. "His parents found him in his room. His neck was broken."

"I'm so sorry," I tell her. I blink at the apple in my hand, realizing that I actually still have a lock on it. "How do I take the light away?"

She comes to me and grabs my free hand, facing the palm up.

"Relax your muscles, not your mind. In your head, pretend you're disposing the apple in a garbage can."

I look straight ahead and act like I spot a trashcan in front of me. I toss the apple into open air towards it. It vanishes in midair- without a bright, shining light.

"Excellent. I'm impressed," Ms. Bell compliments me.

I smile.

For another two hours, Ms. Bell makes me practice forming different, small things. She made me practice on colors. I had to make a pink hat, blue crayon, and a red bracelet. Then she had me practicing scents. I made a rose, sunflower, and perfume. Feeling was the hardest. I couldn't get the Playdo to feel right; it always came out too hard or too soft to where it's sticky. Silk was simple- I was wearing a silk shirt at the moment. Sand came in a quick second. After thirty minutes of learning how to deposit my creations without having to throw them in invisible garbage cans, and without the light, I wanted to cut open my head, take out my brain, and switch it with one that isn't turning into a migraine. I could barely *think* of how to walk down the stairs.

At the door, Ms. Bell pulls me into a hug. I stiffen automatically, but I don't know if she even noticed. It felt awkward, we don't touch much expect maybe a hand on my arm. Once she let me go, I step back quickly.

"Call me if you need anything or have any questions. See you tomorrow," she says goodbye and leaves.

Tomorrow? I think to myself. This is worse than last time. I see her all week instead of once. This is strange, because I should want to punch a wall. But instead, it's as if I'm…alright with it.

Boy, I wonder how long this feeling is going to last.

CHAPTER 7

The next day after school, I get home quicker than I did yesterday. I try to finish up all my homework before Ms. Bell gets here, but I only get through Algebra 2 and Chemistry. French and English will just have to wait.

This morning, I had woken up to green, sticky notes clinging to my wall, my mirror, and my closet door.

The one on my closet I noticed first as I was about to open it and pull out some clothes. The handwriting was definitely female and small. I read the note.

What color was your apple yesterday?

I squint at the words. I didn't even eat an apple yesterday. Who put this here? Islamiat? The handwriting is too clean to be Saultan. I highly doubt its Jamui. I rip the note off my closet.

After choosing my outfit, I go to my dresser to lay it out and change. Hanging over my dresser is a large mirror. Hanging from the mirror is another suspicious green, sticky note. This one said something different.

You made it yourself. Think.

My eyebrows scrunch together as I narrow my eyes at the note, ranking my brain for the meaning. Maybe I'm a little slow but it just about took forever for yesterday's events to rush back into my head. The appearance of Ms. Bell, creating the apple, learning how to break away from the bright light. It all came back in one and stung my head in the process. At first, I thought it was only a dream I had, but I was smarter than that. It actually happened.

After dressing, I step towards my bathroom to find another note on the wall by the door. Just two words this time.

Don't forget.

I won't be forgetting, I promise myself.

Ms. Bell and I meet back in the library for tutoring.

I sit back in my seat and watch, curious, as she sets a piece of paper on the round table in front of me.

"I want you," she begins, "to form a pencil and write an essay about why there should be school."

"Are you kidding me?" I ask. Her hard stare told me she isn't. "Why?"

"To teach you to keep your creation going long and strong. Start now."

This is exactly like school, I think as I remember yellow wood, a pointy end, hard and strong but breakable with power, and at the bottom: pink, soft, with pink contents coming off when you rub it. The smell: wood. The writings DIXON TICONDEROGA. And the number 2 close to the eraser, indicating that's it a number 2 pencil.

A perfect, sharp pencil jumps in my right hand. I begin my essay.

At my third paragraph, explaining my second reason why school is good for us, my pencil is feeling weak and the lead is disappearing way too fast. Then it breaks in two.

Ms. Bell takes my half-done essay and rips it to shreds. She smacks another one down on the table.

I stare down at my broken pencil and say goodbye in my brain. It dies away. I form a stronger one and keep my brain on it and not on my essay. It goes well, except my essay isn't as great. Ms. Bell takes it anyway. I send away my pencil and Ms. Bell folds my essay and puts it in her pocket.

"Create a cellphone," orders Ms. Bell.

I think of my IPhone in my back pocket. Size: flat and tall. Color: the case red. Touch: smooth. There's a button towards the bottom, one on the top, two on the left side. Two holes on the bottom, one to charge and one to stick earphones in. The screen holds a picture of a rose.

I touch my new identical IPhone and show it to Ms. Bell.

"Good- really good," she said. "Call me."

I do as she said, having memorized her number.

Ms. Bell's phone rings from her pocket. Quietly, she takes it out and flips it open. Without a word, she places it in the middle of the table. She sits down in the seat opposite of me and watches. I know I'm not supposed to hang up. She wants to know how long I'll go with keeping the cellphone alive or even in one piece.

It takes precisely fifty minutes until I begin to feel a side effect. My eyes start to water, and it isn't because Ms. Bell and I are having a staring contest. I try to blink and close my eyes, but the tears wouldn't stop from falling off my cheeks. And then my feet go to sleep, but instead they felt dead. My mouth starts shaking, even though I'm not scared or cold. My gums burn in my mouth as if my bottom teeth just got shattered. Tears fall into my free hand and on my lap. I take my eyes away from Ms. Bell and bring them to my hand that feels like it's on fire. I stare at the uncontrollable tears diving into my palm and find a red one smack into my hand. It's my blood. More come down in a free fall. My arms feel as heavy as a house. I drop my phone as my arms fall to my sides. It explodes while falling and disappears in a blazing light. I push my chair back to stand, not able to pick up my arms to catch the blood dripping out of my eyes.

Ms. Bell leaps out of her seat with a bottle, bluish liquid swimming inside. She runs to me, opens the lid, and puts it to my lips. It smells like medicine and it burns my nose. I swallow instantly, begging- no praying- that it will work and I won't black out.

Slow-moving, my feet wake up and my arms don't feel as heavy as they were. My gums stop burning and my mouth stops shaking after. Finally, the tears end, leaving a long, bloody line on each of my cheeks. I crumble back into my seat, more exhausted than I've ever felt.

I don't move while Ms. Bell squints into my eyes very closer. She surveys both my hands and I open my mouth for her to inspect. I lean back when she steps away.

I sense her eyes on me. "That was fifty minutes. Almost an hour," she affirms. "That's the longest it goes and you almost beat it."

I was too drained to acknowledge what she just said.

Ms. Bell lets me lean on her as she helps me into my room and on my bed. She opens the window a bit to let air breathe in and leaves a glass of water on my dresser as if to help me prepare for my hangover. How sweet.

I allow myself to sleep.

The next day, I rush through my homework, filling in answers that have nothing to do with the questions. I just wanted to get it out of the way.

Once Ms. Bell gets here, and we enter the library together, she has me open my hands far out and three inches away from each other.

"Why?" I ask, feeling awkward.

She steps back. "You're going to form a ruler."

"Okay."

I close my eyes. Size: twenty-five inches, flat as a whiteboard, as fat as my two fingers. Color: light, dirty brown. Words: inch. 1-25. (Yeah, that sounds about right.) Touch: rough, hard. Scent: dirt and wood. The wood is stronger than a pencil, but less strength than the wall in your room.

A long, tough ruler appears in my out stretched hands, numbers scribbled on the sides.

"Very good," Ms. Bell nods at my work. Without speaking, she takes it from my hands and smashes the ruler into the wall behind me. The ruler makes a hole in the wall as big as a baseball. The ruler is still in one piece.

Okay, so maybe a ruler is stronger than a wall. Or at least mine is.

"And very strong," Ms. Bell said. "Your brain is powerful."

"My brain is powerful?" I repeat.

"Yes, powerful enough to make something stronger than it's meant to be." She holds up the ruler. "You could make this into a weapon."

"Why would I want to?" I ask, my tone sharper than I meant it to be.

She shrugs. "Just a thought."

I look at the floor. "May I ask you something?"

"Yes," she smiles. The smile encourages me to keep going.

"What do you guys expect me to do with this ability?" it's still kind of hard to admit I have an ability like this.

Ms. Bell silently looks around the room, as if to make sure no one else is listening. "To keep you safe from Ike Henderson."

"Oh..."

"Mariam, we *both* work with the police. They know you're in on this and that Ike might try to hurt you but they know nothing about your gift. Actually, they have no clue this gift even exists, no idea that that's the reason that Ike is killing those innocent kids. That's just a secret between you, me, Shelly, and Dr. Jeff. If you don't want them to find out about you, we won't let them."

"So, they know who I am and that he murdered my sister?"

"Yes," she answers. "They know who you are. They know what he did to your sister and what he did to you. They know he could possibly come back for you," she says, looking me over for a reaction. I hide my fear way behind my eyes.

"Will he come back for me?" I ask just to see what Ms. Bell will say.

She licks her lips. "I don't know. But we're here, just in case."

I look down at the floor.

"If we hurry now, we can get done early," Ms. Bell tells me.

I nod.

The rest of the hour, I make a mini fridge. The ice inside wasn't as cold and melted in your hands right away. I made a hairbrush, except I invented it to smell like sunflowers- Ms. Bell thought it was impressive. We ended off with making a purple and pink backpack.

Ms. Bell leaves an hour earlier. I eat dinner this time with my siblings and watch T.V. with Islamiat. I help Saultan with his homework, too lazy to do the rest of mine.

Once I get upstairs to my room, I was close to passing out. I noticed my phone blinking, trying to grab my attention so I could check the new messages and voice mails. I completely ignore it. I pull on my bed clothes and climb into bed. I shut off my light.

My phone rings.

And rings.

And rings.

Over and over again. Whoever needs to talk to me is desperate. But I was never this tired before. I shut off my phone and fall asleep.

CHAPTER 8

"What the hell!"

The voice makes me jump instantly. I look up from staring at my greasy pizza in the noisy cafeteria to find Ashley glaring daggers at me with that look that says I better have a good reason.

"What did I do?" I ask, confused.

She slams her bottom on the seat across from me with May following her movement. "What did you do? *What did you do*?" she repeats again, with more force that she's starting to scare me. "Where were you yesterday, Mariam? And I better hear a good excuse." How did I know she was going to say that?

"I was at home," I answer, totally confused.

"Not good enough. Where the heck were you for May's *surprise birthday party*?"

My eyes widen from realizing my stupid mistake, but I don't speak.

"What, now you remember?" she said.

"Oh my gosh- Ashley I'm so sorry-" I try to apologize.

Ashley holds up a hand in front of my face. "Save it. I'm not the one you should be apologizing to."

I look at May. Her eyes are wide and on my face. Her hands are trembling. I can tell she hates these emotions going on around the table. She doesn't know how to handle them, how to work with them. And it's my fault she has this problem. If I had just paid attention yesterday instead of helping myself. I ruined her birthday.

I look her straight in the eye. "May, I am so sorry."

Her jaw tightens and I want to punch myself. "It's okay."

I shake my head. "No, it's not."

"Damn right it's not," Ashley snaps. "How stupid do you think we looked? When we got there, the guests were all standing outside pissed because they couldn't get in- because *you* weren't there."

"I'm sorry Ashley."

"Sorry is not good enough. Ever since the date with Dillon you've been distant. You practically ignore us."

"That's not true," May attempts to defend me, only she's not that great of a lawyer.

"May, *stop* being so soft," Ashley barks the words in her face.

May looks away, because this time, she isn't joking.

"You don't answer our phone calls," Ashley continues, "you hardly say a word at lunch, and you run before we can catch you after school. It's like you don't want to be friends anymore."

That's not true, I think of saying. I don't know why I kept my mouth shut.

Ashley's voice calms a bit as she says, "Look Mariam, I'm trying to help you get your life back together because of the loss of you sister. You're making it very hard."

I didn't like what she said. The words that came out of her mouth gave me the impression that she thought I was weak. That thought was like alcohol, because the next words that sprouted out of my mouth I could not stop and I had no clue why I said them.

"*You're* trying to get my life back together?" I spit in her face. "I don't need your help getting my life back together. I never needed any of your guy's help. I'm perfectly fine on my own."

Ashley raises her eyebrows at me as if I just called her stupid. But before that, her whole face had fallen, her eyes turning sad and her throat tightening up. The look in her eyes resembled May's. For that quick moment, Ashley was a little kid being told that who she thought was her best friend, never gave two craps about her. But then that was gone and the mask fell over her face again.

"Oh you don't, do you? Fine. If you don't want your friends there for you to try to help you out, then we'll leave you *perfectly* alone. C'mon May," Ashley ends the argument by standing up.

May looks from Ashley to me. Her blue eyes beg me to ask for forgiveness. That's not going to happen.

"May, didn't you hear her?" Ashley urges her. "Mariam doesn't need us."

"May, that's not what I said," I attempt.

"That's exactly what she said."

Slowly, May steps onto her feet and follows behind Ashley to the cafeteria doors. I stare down at the table, but out of the corner of my eye, I see May's blond waves flip and flop as she turns to look at me. I ignore her and face a fact.

I messed up.

After school, I decided I needed time to think. Your probably saying, "Think *what*, you need to go apologize!" but I and saying sorry don't work together. I can't remember the last time I said sorry and really meant it.

Anyhow, I turn my course and walk on the trail that would lead me behind the school. It's still winter and cold as ever. My jacket isn't helping much. This is the longest way to my driver, a warm car with warm seats, but I can survive in this temperature for a moment. There's ice on the ground, basically snow. I wonder if it'll snow this Christmas. Saultan and Islamiat would like that.

Once I get to the left side of the high school, walking towards the corner, I notice two voices shouting back and forth. Quietly, I peek my head over the side of the wall, recognizing the two figures immediately.

Dillon and Nelci both look angry. Actually, Nelci looks beyond angry and Dillon looks more annoyed. His girlfriend is standing on her tip-e-toes, trying her best to beat his height. She couldn't. I do my finest shot at listening to what Dillon's saying, the only one who wants to keep his voice low. Nelci's just yelling away.

"You can't just end it like this, Dillon!" Nelci screams, her ugly, brown hair flying through the air.

"I just did," he says back, his voice leveled.

"Why are you doing this? Don't you love me?"

"Of course not- I only *liked* you," Dillon said.

"Who else is there?" she suddenly asks.

"What- no one," he says, but his face gives him away.

"No one instead of Miss Loser!"

"Nelci, I have no idea who that is."

"Yes you do!"

"No I do not."

"You know what," she pushes his chest, tripping off her toes, "you want to break up, then we'll break up!"

"That's what I've been trying to tell you."

"Oh, shut up!" she screams. She walks away from him- towards me. I ditch my spot, turn around, and run back the way I came. I forget the path I chose and go the regular direction.

I felt like doing a cartwheel and the splits. I couldn't stop smiling.

Their relationship is over.

It's over.

It's over.

"Now, we both know your creations are not real," says Ms. Bell, walking in circles around me as I sit in a chair. "If you don't keep your mind on it, it will disappear and everyone will forget it was there. Today, I'm going to teach you how to leave your mark." I stand up as she pushes a different, empty chair in front of me.

"I need you to create a sword," she speaks behind me. "Make sure it's sharp."

I close my eyes. Size: longer than a man's arm, skinny as a folder, one end as sharp as a needle, the other end as a handle. Touch: flat part of the blade is smooth, sharp, rough and metal. The sword appears in my opened hand. It's heavy and I almost drop it. The blade is pointy and glistens when the sun hits it through the windows. Ms. Bell stands behind the empty chair, her hands behind her back.

"Your next move is to cut this chair in half," said Ms. Bell.

Finally we get to have some fun. I pull the sword all the way up over my head and slam it down into the chair. The sword slices through it, treating it like bread. The two slashed pieces fall apart, loudly clattering onto the hardwood.

"Good job," Ms. Bell says. "Take away the sword."

Once I do, I watch with amazement as the broken chair quickly fixes itself back together. Invisible hands lift up the two halves and stick them together. A light with glitter dazzles around it, gluing it back together. The light disappears, showing the chair better than it was before I attacked it with my sword.

"H-how?" I stutter, confused.

"No cause- no effect," she explains. "If you take away the cause of the problem, it never happened."

"How am I supposed to keep an effect without the cause?" I ask. "Seems impossible."

"Not impossible. All you have to do is think of the chair being broken in half as you throw your weapon away," she demonstrates.

I raise my eyebrows, surprised. "Is that it?"

"It's not as easy as it sounds. You need to make sure not to think of anything else or your brain will be confused and hurt you. Just take short breaths," she adds. Those words of advice remind me of when she used to be my therapist. I don't miss those days; this is a lot better.

I close my eyes to concentrate better. I think of the sword again, clutching it tightly in my hand when it comes. I take short breaths, trying to relax my mind. I didn't feel like having my head hurt today.

In a quick second, I cut the chair in half. Two more short breaths. I throw away the sword and quickly start to think. First of the two words "broken chair". I think it over and over. While I'm thinking of it, I make a picture of the chair cut in half in my head. Easier than I thought it would be.

Then Dillon's beautiful face pops into my head. Dimples. Stunning eyes like the sunset. The whole view of him releases butterflies in my stomach.

My brain burns in my forehead, so hard I cry out in pain. I grab my head, wanting to claw out my hair. With my eyes still squeezed shut, I feel Ms. Bell place her hand on my shoulder and press a cold, glass cup against my lips. I recognize the heavy scent. I open my mouth wide to let some medicine flow down my throat instead of letting out a scream. The liquid falls down my mouth fast. Immediately, the pain stops. I open my eyes.

The chair's on the ground in half. And the sword's gone. I have an effect without the cause!

Ms. Bell's smiling. "Good job. Well, almost good job. This explains why your math test appeared blank- you took away the pencil that you wrote with. And you created the dress in the mall, also the tag. You took away the dress and the tag, it disappears from the receipt and it's like you never bought the dress. Look at the wall."

I turn the way she points. The wall looks normal, like every other inch of the room. I shrug at Ms. Bell.

"Remember I broke it with the ruler. There was a hole and now there isn't."

"Wow," I say, deeply amazed. "I never noticed."

"I knew you wouldn't."

"So, if I wanted people to forget about what I had just made, all I have to do is make sure not to leave an effect?"

"Not exactly," she says. "You can create anything and show me with my own eyes, with or without an effect, and I'll always remember. Because I taught myself to. You've taught yourself to too. Dr. Jeff remembers too and so does Shelly."

"I guess there's no way to trick you guys," I said, crossing my arms.

"There isn't."

Ten minutes later, after Ms. Bell had disposed the two halves of the chair (don't ask me how), I'm sitting in my seat, my elbows on the table. Ms. Bell takes a blank piece of paper out of her front pocket and unfolds it, setting it on the table in front of me. The crease in the middle of the paper tries to blend in.

"What is it?" I ask, clueless while staring at the plain paper.

"*This* is your essay about why there should be school," she answers.

I blink at the paper. "But I wrote a whole page…oh. Right," I sigh, finally understanding. I wrote all of that and now it's gone.

"Exactly. Rewrite it."

"All of it!" I ask. Nope, I won't, I thought.

"*All* of it."

Fine.

I sigh in frustration and order a sharpened pencil to form in my hand.

The next few minutes, I write my reasons about why there should be boring school. Keeping the pencil in my hand is super easy. The last part, keeping my essay on the paper, was hard.

I had to retry *four* times, twice Dillon or Ashley disturbed my thinking, burning my brain. Once I only got one paragraph to stay on the paper. The last time, I was too weak to concentrate. After Ms. Bell caught me trying to fall asleep, she said practice is over even though she knew something is wrong- even asked.

"Nothing," I lie.

Ms. Bell blocks the door. "I remember when I was your age. I was always in fights with my parents and friends. I never did anything right."

I sigh slowly and lean against the round table closest to the door. "My friends don't think I need them anymore."

"Why would they think that?" she wonders.

"Well, I *have* been ignoring them a little. I totally ruined May's birthday surprise party. And I might've said I never needed them in my life," I admit. At the end, I shrug my shoulders as if I don't know why I told her all that.

"Don't you think you should tell them why?"

I shrug again. "What am I supposed to say? They know nothing about all of this."

"Tell them what you know will make it better. You don't have to tell them the whole truth; just enough to assure them you still need them. You don't want to lose your friends," she says, power in her voice. A power I like.

I feel myself smile a little. "I thought you weren't supposed to be my therapist any longer?"

"Well you asked for my advice," she said.

"I did not…"

Ms. Bell grins at me and I roll my eyes.

After saying goodbye to Ms. Bell and locking myself in my room to dress for bed, I look at Madison sitting, her hair hiding behind her shoulders, on my dresser. Dillon gave me her to remind me of the memories we had. I turn around and stare at the photo in the white frame on my nightstand. The photo of my sleepover with Ashley and May. Our mouths are stuffed with popcorn, our eyes shining, and arms over each other's shoulders. My tenth birthday.

Ashley and May are the only great friends I have…or had. Anyway, they were the people that understood me, the one's I could tell all my problems to and they wouldn't judge me.

And I lost them because I'm only paying attention to someone who isn't alive.

And won't be coming back.

CHAPTER 9

The ringing from my phone wakes me up Saturday morning. I open my caked lids and reach over for my phone on the nightstand. I don't bother looking at the caller.

"Hello?" I answer.

"Get dressed," Shelly speaks into my ear. "We're going on a field trip."

She hangs up and I find the clock to the right: 8:20. Really Shelly, this early? On a *Saturday*?

I fall out of bed and crawl into the shower. It feels like I'm in there for too long, but after I get out, lotion, and dress, Agent Clark is just pulling up. I tie my hair and pull on a jacket. Inside Shelly's little bug, she has a pink box of glazed donuts. She offers me the rest.

Once she gets on the freeway, nowhere towards her office, I get suspicious.

"Where are we headed?" I question.

"A neighborhood some miles away," she answers.

"Why?"

"Suzette Morales. This morning, she was found dead in her room with a gap in her heart."

I swallow. "How old?"

"Eleven. Before we get to the crime scene, you need to promise *never* to let this information get out. Don't tell your family or your closes friends. Don't write it in your diary. No one knows about this except the family and the police."

"How do you get the parents not to speak about it?"

Shelly licks her lips. "We lie to them."

"What? But-"

"We tell them that the murderer will hurt them and the rest of the family if they ever tell anyone," she said.

"And they believe you?"

"Of course. Especially if they have other children."

"How can you just lie to them? Doesn't that scare them for the rest of their lives?"

"I'm not the one that tells them. I just look for evidence at the scene."

"Why are you taking me with you?" I ask.

"Because you're a part of this now. And it's good to have another pair of eyes on my side."

On your side, I thought. Who's on the other side?

"Well, I promise I won't tell anyone," I said.

"Good, because those fat officers are probably going to be *really* mad that I brought a teen to a crime scene."

It takes a while to get to the destination. The houses are fairly small but they're given a lot of land to work with. Most seem to use it to grow gardens or create a friendly play area for kids. But each house got a nice size property.

The house we stop at is beautiful.

There's a white picket fence and stone pathway leading up to the white door. It's a thin two-story house, the color a pale blue, the window frames white and the grass a grand dark green.

Shelly parks on the side of the road. There are no police cars but white vans and black trucks. I follow her to the fence, which she unlatches and pushes to the side. I trail closely behind her as we walk over the pathway and right through the opened front door.

The noise and smells hit me all at once. Someone crying, whispers, feet shuffling upstairs. The strong smell of smoke, coffee, and cheap perfume. I have the knowledge knowing that this isn't usually how the house is. I imagine the crying switch to laughter, the scent of smoke actually cookies. The coffee is really lemonade and the cheap perfume belongs to a little girl as she turns herself into a princess.

That imagination shatters when Shelly grabs my arm and tugs me past a woman weeping on a couch. Used tissues are around her feet and a man with a beard has his hand on her leg. He pats it every three seconds and water in his eyes trickle out slowly. There's a lady and man watching them while they lean against the wall. There are holsters at their waists, holsters with guns. Shelly finds the stairs and we climb them to the top.

Just like downstairs, there are armed men and woman leaning against the two sides of the walls throughout the whole hallway. They're heads are straight but their eyes roam around, locking on your face and watching your hands. I don't know if they're expecting a gun to appear or someone to bust out with some wicked karate moves. I keep my head down. I'm not supposed to be here but they might think I'm an adult by my height. I'm only a little shorter than Shelly, who's holding her head up like she owns the country.

We step inside a girl's room. The wallpaper is blue with daises. There's a small fan and a lamp with stickers on the pale shade. The curtains are white and dusty, the bed's blue and there's a full mirror on the closet. There's an IPod on the floor by a desk and a chair, still playing music into the earphones, minutes until the battery runs out and goes dark. There's also a T.V. and pictures clinging to a peg board. Someone's inspecting the rug with a magnifying glass and a woman is reaching under the bed, searching for clues. I stand by the dresser, staring…at the body on the floor.

"Don't look," Shelly whispers in my ear.

"Too late," I whisper back. My mouth is oddly dry. It wasn't like that thirty seconds ago.

Her head is the only part that shows from under the sheet. Pretty, black, curly hair. The blood is still there, dark and sinking deeper and deeper into the carpet, like a puddle of wine. Why did they leave the eyes open? Her eyes are a light brown as they stare back at me. *Stop him*, they tell me*, or every other kid that's like you will turn out like me.*

My hands begin to shake so I hide them in my pockets.

Agent Clark circles around the dead girl- Suzette Morales- and bends down on her knees by the woman who was searching under the bed.

"How deep is the hole?" asks Shelly.

"Just puncturing the heart," is her answer. "She bled out."

"Sign of a struggle?"

"Right wrist is bruised. The mom says she doesn't sleep well at night. My guess is," the detective goes on, "when he came in through the window, she was up and tried to get away. She was probably able to jump out of bed, but he grabbed her wrist and forced her around. And then he stabbed her. But the cut wasn't exactly deep."

"Maybe something interrupted." It was the man with the magnifying glass who spoke.

"Like what?"

"Well," Shelly speaks up, "if she noticed someone climbing into her room, she must've screamed a lot. He had to hurry because her parents were waking up."

"But if he had to hurry," says the woman, "I'm pretty sure he had no time to perfectly set the window screen back up."

The detective stands up and Shelly follows her to the window by the bed. I scoot closer to them both. The window is all the way up. The detective pushes at the screen some.

"It's like it was never tampered with," the detective said.

"I'm guessing he crawled up using that," Agent Clark points at the overhead shading the patio.

"Exactly. He climbed up, took off the screen, opened the window, and came right in."

Opened the window and came right in? Then that means…

"The alarm went off," I mutter to myself.

The man had good ears. "What?"

Shelly and the detective look at me.

"The alarm. He had to hurry because the alarm went off," I said.

"But they don't have an alarm-"

"Excuse me, who are you?" the woman detective wants to know.

Agent Clark jumps in front of her. "She's my apprentice. She's going to college for criminal justice. She wants to grow up and be *just* like you."

The compliment calms the detective down. She sighs. "Go on."

I look at the man.

"They don't have an alarm," he repeats. "Nothing went off when he opened the window."

"Because he didn't use it," I say, only now realizing what type of murderer Ike is.

"Explain," the detective orders. Shelly nods at me.

"He came in through the front door and up the stairs."

I look down at the IPod and earphones on the floor. "She wasn't in bed. She was listening to her music at her desk."

I notice how the small T.V. is angled to give you a view of the door. "She saw the door open from the T.V. screen. She realized it wasn't a family member and ducked when he came at her. The IPod dropped out of her hands."

The rug placed in front of the bed isn't straight like it should be. There's a bump in the middle. "She did try to make a run for the door and he did grab her wrist."

"But why wasn't the wound deep?" Shelly queries.

I lick my lips and catch a pair of green eyes watching from inside the closest.

"Because she bit him," I point.

At that moment, a young beagle squeezes out of the doorway of the closest and runs to Shelly. She gets on her knees and pets the dog as it tastes her fingers.

"B-but," the detective stutters, "the mom never said anything about a dog."

Shelly stands up and the beagle jogs around her legs. "I'm sure the mom didn't have much to say with her daughter being killed."

The detective shuts her mouth and checks inside the closest for clues. I edge my way beside Agent Clark.

"Good job, Miss Wilson," she pats my arm. The beagle licks Shelly's dark brown boots with her pink tongue.

"Thanks."

"How did you know he used the front door?" Shelly asked.

I stare at the floor. "This man attacked my sister in board daylight. Anyone could've been watching out their window and I was right there. He doesn't care how he gets the job done; he thinks he can get out of anything."

Agent Clark's looking right at me. "Your eyes are better than I expected."

I smile.

"Evidence!" the detective calls out.

She comes out of the closest with a ripped strip from a pair of jeans. Dog teeth mark the edges. The beagle barks happily at my feet.

"What the hell are we supposed to do with that?" the man asks.

"At least it's something," she says back.

"Definitely not much. We need a team to check the front door handle just to make sure this is *the* Ike Henderson we're looking for."

Shelly takes my arm. "Let's search outside."

I trail behind Shelly and the beagle follows me. The woman's still crying and the dog abandons us to lick her owner's feet. Once outside, Shelly searches around the rose bushes and under windows.

"I wish I had brought my magnifying glass along with me," she complains at one point.

I stare off to the side. The handle is as long as my middle finger and fat as a marker. Touch: smooth and made out of glass. The glass is see-through and sleek.

"Here you go."

I open my palm to show her the magnifying glass. Shelly gives me a strange but appraising look before taking it out of my hand.

"You're getting a lot better," she compliments.

I shrug. "I know."

She chuckles and uses it for the next ten minutes as I follow her around like a shadow. When she gives it back, I make it go away.

"Nothing?" I question.

She shakes her head. "I shouldn't be surprised- he never leaves evidence. Grace is right about that piece of fabric from his jeans- at least it's something."

"The detective?"

She nods.

There's a loud screech as a black truck does a risky turn onto this street and the driver stomps on the brakes right before slamming into Shelly's precious yellow beetle. The car shuts off and four figures step out.

"Crap," Shelly mumbles.

"What's the problem?" I ask, stepping closer to her side without realizing it.

"*That's* the problem," Shelly points with her chin.

I look at the one particular figure she's glaring at. He slams shut the driver's door and steps onto Suzette Morales's property. He's tall like a basketball player, with a long chin and heavy eyebrows. His brown locks are layered all over, the top layers jagged cut. The locks are long enough with the ability to sweep it back or down. Dark shades hide his eyes and his nice body works a black suit correctly as if he was born in it.

He stops in the middle of the yard and takes off his sunglasses to survey the crowd, revealing dark blue eyes. He drops the sunglasses inside his breast pocket.

"Alright people, you can head on home now," he says, his voice innocent but demanding. "We have this place taken care of."

Agent Clark rolls her eyes while the other few detectives or officers look confused.

The man with his magnifying glass is suddenly beside Shelly. "What is *he* doing here?"

"What do you think?" said Shelly. She turns to me. "Just keep quiet."

"Ok," I said.

Right after I say that, the new guy lays his eyes on Shelly. He smiles. He starts walking this way, his companions, two men and a woman, trailing behind him. Shelly stands up straighter, bracing herself. The magnifying-glass man stays where he is.

He stops in front of her. "Wow Shelly. You're even more gorgeous than the last time I remember."

"Well thank you, Malcolm," she says, stiffly.

He slowly smiles. "I'm just kidding."

Shelly smiles also, but hers is nowhere near kind. "I see you still drive like a drunken bastard."

"Only so that you'll know that I'm here and in charge."

"I couldn't care less where you are."

"Awe, still heartbroken?"

"Every morning I wake up and realize: damn, you were a real stupid mistake."

Malcolm laughs, mouth wide open, eyes shut tight and head up. "You're cute when you lie."

"Oh, so now I'm cute?"

He sighs then and his smile falls off his face. "Where is it?"

"Where's what?" Shelly asks.

"Don't play dumb with me. I have ears everywhere."

"I don't know what you mean."

Malcolm groans. "Where is the evidence?"

"Oh, that," she says, pretending to remember. "Yeah- you can't have it."

He steps closer to her. His lips are near her ear, the ear on my side. His words might only be for her, but I can hear them just as fine. "Stop playing games with me. What's yours is mine."

"Ha! That rule ended when I kicked you out."

Shelly steps away from him and crosses her arms.

We all hear the front door shut and Malcolm twists around in a hurry. Grace moves across our view, heading towards the white van with something in her hand.

"Hey, you there!" Malcolm shouts to her.

Grace turns around.

"Let me see that. Give it to me," he holds out his hand for the only evidence against Ike Henderson in a plastic bag.

"Grace, don't!" Shelly yells. "We found it. It's ours not his."

"It's *ours*?" Malcolm repeats to Shelly, confused with his arm still up. "What's that supposed to me, Shelly? We're both on the same side."

"That's bull and you know it, Malcolm."

One of Malcolm's men, a guy with bulky arms, snatches the plastic bag out of Grace's hand and tosses it to Malcolm. Malcolm catches it with his left hand and holds it up to his face to peer into it. Shelly groans loudly and makes an attempt to reach for the priceless evidence but the bulky guy holds her arm to hold her back.

"It's *ours* Malcolm," Shelly said. "I can hold this against you."

"Please, you're not even a real cop," he said.

"I have a badge."

"So does my nine year old nephew."

Shelly grumbles, glaring at Malcolm like she can't wait to be released so she can rip his head off with her teeth.

Malcolm lowers the evidence from his face, setting his eyes on me. He's curious.

"Who's that?" he asks.

"My apprentice," Shelly answers with her lips curled in a snarl. "She's in college."

"Yeah, right."

He tucks the evidence in his breast pocket, right beside his glasses, and comes towards me. I brace myself, standing up straighter like Shelly did. He stops in front of me and I expect to hear a snort or to roll his eyes. Instead, he holds out his hand and lightly smiles. I give him my hand.

"Malcolm West," he introduces. "And you are?"

"Mariam Wilson," I said. "Are you a detective too?"

"No. I work with the FBI. And I'm sure you don't go to college, do you?"

I ignore the nodding Shelly's doing with her head. For some reason, I don't want to lie to Malcolm West. "No, I don't. I'm only a junior."

Grace gasps, looking hurt, but Malcolm smiles even bigger while Shelly contemplates on ripping my head off instead.

"What is a junior like you doing at a crime scene?"

"She's really good at this detective stuff," speaks up the magnifying-glass man for the first time since Malcolm stood in front of us. "She found the evidence."

"The evidence you stole," Shelly throws in, finally wrenching her hand out of the bulky man's grasp.

Malcolm ignores her. "It's *your* evidence? *You* found it?"

"Well, Grace got it out of the closest-" I try to explain.

"She found it," Grace interrupts, expressionless as if bored.

"Hm," Malcolm looks me up and down. "Well, I'll make sure to keep very good care of it for you."

"You're an idiot, Malcolm," remarks Shelly.

Malcolm turns to her. "You know what Shelly, I really miss the words you used to whisper in my ear. What were they again? Super-model-hot-and-gorgeous? Or was it just sexy?"

Did Shelly just blush?

"Go jump off a cliff," she says. Maybe that redness that rose in her cheeks wasn't embarrassment, but anger. "No one will miss you."

"No one expect you, baby."

"You wish."

Malcolm turns to his three partners. "This is our scene now." He switches around to face us and the other few detectives standing outside. "This is our scene now, people! You can go home to your families. Move it along!"

The detectives look unsure at first, wondering who Malcolm thought he was exactly. But soon, they pick up their things and head to their white vans parked on the curb. Grace waves goodbye to Shelly, joining the leaving party. The magnifying-glass man goes with her. The only ones who stay are the officers with the parents and the guards that stood along the hallways upstairs.

"Shouldn't we be leaving too?" I whisper in Shelly's ear.

She only bites her upper lip, staring Malcolm down intently. He smiles and reaches for her arm. Shelly doesn't move away. He takes her arm and pulls her close. They aren't touching, but she has to look up to see his face better.

"You need to go home," he said, keeping her arm in his hand, seeming not to notice. Or perhaps, he just doesn't want to let go. "You should not be here at all."

"Thanks for the concern, but I can take care of myself," she said.

He rolls his eyes. "I'm serious. I don't know what, but this criminal is definitely different from the others we've chased. That rip from his jeans is the best evidence we have ever discovered. I'm sorry for taking it."

"No you're not."

Shelly takes her arm back. She forgets me and walks towards her yellow beetle waiting for her, with her head down. Malcolm watches her go before laying his eyes on me. He doesn't take my arm but nods at me.

"Nice meeting you, Mariam. Take care of Shelly for me. She doesn't have anybody else."

The ride to drop me off at home is painful. The radio is shut off and little squirts of water beats against the windows. I wish the weather was better so that I could lean my head out the window with the sun heating the side of my face. Then I could sleep and dream without having to listen to Shelly tightening and untightening her grip on the poor steering wheel.

I open my mouth with a conversation on mind, but surely not the one Agent Clark will be happy to talk about.

"You and Malcolm used to be together?"

Shelly tenses up. "Something like that."

"You used to live in the same house," I say, as a statement.

"Yes," she answers anyway.

"Only couples live in the same house together. Unless you were friends with benefits…"

Shelly looks at me sideways. I decide to shut my mouth. Alright, not exactly the best way to keep a steady conversation.

After a while, we make it to my house. The guard lets us through and Shelly parks the car. She leans back in her seat. I stare at her.

"I and Malcolm," she begins, "used to be good to each other. We met at a crime scene looking for clues left by another dumb murderer. What no one knew was that the murderer was still there, hiding in the basement. I volunteered to go down there with Malcolm and two of his men. Once down there, his men were knocked out. Malcolm was pushed to the floor and the criminal shoved me against the wall. He strangled me around the throat with only one hand, cutting off my airway. I couldn't reach my gun. It was so dark I couldn't see anything but I could feel it when he pressed the knife against my skin. The blade was cold."

I'm too frightened and amazed to say anything. She keeps going.

"I thought of one thing and one thing only: my son. I hardly see him once a week and I couldn't believe I hadn't gotten the chance to see him that week yet. That week I was supposed to die.

"Then a shot rang out through the air. The knife clattered to the floor and the murderer fell onto his face. I looked up…and saw Malcolm grasping his gun, the point of it smoking."

Shelly puts her hand on her forehead, staring down at her feet. "He saved my life."

"But then, what happened to you two?" I asked.

She shakes her head like it's unbelievable. "I don't know. After a whole year it's like we woke up and decided to hate each other. We argued and lied to one another. I used to like it when he held me. Now I don't want him near me. He cheated on me. And then I cheated on him because he cheated on me. I'm not proud about that."

"I don't understand. It seemed like he cared about you today," I said. "He wants you to be careful-"

"He always thinks I'm going to do something stupid. He thought that after we broke up that I would quit working in the criminal business because it's his thing. He thought wrong," she said, rubbing her left eye.

I turn my gaze out the window. "Do you think…that the only reason you were together was because you thought you owed him something for saving your life?"

"What I thought was that he was my prince charming," she raises her voice, her shoulders lifting. "My superhero. But he was just doing his job."

"How do you know?"

"Because I woke up and realized that I really didn't love him," she blurts. She looks away, letting out a shaky breath.

I didn't know what else to say. It seemed to get a whole lot tense and Shelly's love life is nowhere near close to my business. They were together and now they aren't. Things change. That horrible thought reminds me of Dillon.

“Thanks for finding the evidence that don’t belong to me anymore,” Shelly said, starting the car. “Don’t expect Ms. Bell today or tomorrow. She’s not feeling well.”

Stop Shelly, I want to say. You can’t forget someone that meant so much to you. I tried it too.

It didn’t work.

CHAPTER 10

On Sunday afternoon, I'm resting in the living room with my head against the cold window as it snows outside. I can see the white snowflakes fall out the corner of my eye. Saultan and Islamiat were excited at the sight of it for the first few hours. They couldn't wait for the ground to be all white and heavy enough for snowball fights and snow angels. But they got tired of waiting for that wish and went upstairs to play. Jamui looked right through the falling snow, stuck in his own world. Then he locked himself in his room. Now it's just me.

The knob on the front door dodders. I look up at it but I don't sit up or lift my feet off the couch. Mom walks in with her keys in hand and a huge, black umbrella frosted with snow. She shakes it clean outside before closing the door and setting it in the basket with the other spare umbrellas. She's wearing a gray snow jacket with the hood up, which she pulls down to show her short, black hair in a tight, strict bun. Under her jacket she has on a dark skirt with stockings and a white, turtleneck sweater. She smiles at me with classic red lips. I smile back and listen to her high heels as she walks away.

I didn't expect Mom to be home right now, this early. She's a heart surgeon at the local hospital and she's basically there morning till night. It's not her fault that her dream job steals a lot of her time. Not only is she a surgeon, she owns a hair salon not far from the elementary school I used to go to. While she was in college, that was the job that helped pay most of the bills. She loves working on hair, creating new styles, each girl that sits in her chair her own personal Barbie Doll. And she was good at it, exactly the reason why the salon now belongs to her.

I remember when I was in the fourth grade and knew Mom was going to be late to pick me up. I always walked the short twelve minutes to the salon. I knew every worker. Claire worked only on Monday's and Friday's. Stacey I only say on Wednesday's and Molly seemed to be there every day. I would stare at Claire's long fingers as they lifted soapy strands of hair up to spray warm water on. Soap would slide down her arm, dangle from the tip of her elbow, and drop onto her toes peeking out from under her sandals. Stacey's fingernails were always painted a hot pink. She would cut hair so fast; the customer would hardly sit in the seat longer than ten minutes. It was fun watching the hot pink flashing through the air with amazing speed with a pair of silver scissors in the right hand. She didn't watch what she was doing either- she would be smiling at me.

Molly was different than the other employees. She had in headphones while she worked, rejecting the music being played throughout the whole salon. I never saw her in anything expect tight blue or black jeans and a gray shirt. She'd grin to herself as if laughing to jokes invisible ghosts are whispering in her ear. She hardly spoke while coloring strands of hair different shades of brown or black or maybe blond. Whenever I walked in, she'd give me that same curious look as if she kept forgetting whose daughter I was.

I look down at my hands. Back then, everything was so simple. I was carefree, Jamui knew how to use his voice, and there was no dead sister. Now I'm hiding from a serial killer, there's a grave holding a three-year-old girl, and kids are dying because they're just a little too special.

I feel myself slide towards the left as someone sits beside me. Mom. She has two cups of tea and hands me one of them. It smells like honey. I take a sip and the liquid burns my tongue.

Mom moves my braids out of my face. "What's the matter?"

I shake my head. "Nothing."

She pulls my chin up. "I know when something's wrong with my girl. Tell me."

How did I ever think I could lie to her?

I meet her gaze. Can I really tell her everything that's been going on? That Ms. Bell isn't trying to teach me math or science, but how to master a gift my little sister threw at me? Should I even tell her about the special power I have? Will it scare her if she finds out I'm working with the police and saw a dead body yesterday? Will she get angry, not because I'm keeping this huge secret from her, but because I could get myself killed? Or will she protect me from Ike Henderson like I wish she could?

She touches my arm and I realize she's still waiting for me to tell her the truth.

"I'm…I'm failing math," I admit. "I can't join volleyball."

I must keep her safe. To tell her the secret is to strip away the cement wall that's keeping her guarded.

She pulls me closer to her and I drop my head on her shoulder while her arm goes around my own shoulders. She pats my head, comforting me in a way I can't get enough of.

"It's okay," she tells me. "You'll get your grade up and the coach will *have* to let you on the team. They can't win without you."

I smile. "I wish it was easy said than done."

"Hey, look at me."

She moves her arm away and I look at her.

"I didn't raise a loser, did I?"

"No," I say.

"That's right. We Wilson's are winners. We were made to succeed. Look where we are, where we're living. This type of money isn't just lying on the floor. Your father and I have worked hard to get where we are. And you're going to have to work hard to get what *you* want."

Volleyball falls to the last thing on my mind as I remember the bigger problem. "What happens if the thing I'm trying hard to do is dangerous?"

Mom purses her lips together and thinks first. "If it's for the right reasons, then you keep trying. But be careful. Sometimes to succeed that right reason, you have to do something wrong."

Like lose my two best friends? The thought of them makes me sad. I choke back the upcoming tears.

Mom entwines her fingers with mine. "Don't cry, Mariam. Tell me what type of daughter I raised."

"A winner."

I'm running down a dark alley, toward the little girl calling my name with a weak voice. The closer I get to her, the father he drags her away. Her screams echo through the air, her breath makes my heart drum faster because the sound changes every time. Getting dimmer. She's dying.

A wall appears in front of me. I run into it, as if expecting it to break. My breath comes out fast and loud, every cell in my body pumping with energy. I squeeze my eyes shut as I listen to her scream out in pain over and over again.

I tell myself to wake up.

I don't.

I struggle up the wall, around it, under. I punch at it with all I've got, my knuckles bleeding and burning. I hear her shout out my name with her little voice. She tells me to help her, but I know I can't.

God, I didn't know anyone could scream so loud.

I drop to my hands and knees and beg him to stop. I yell at him that I'll do anything if he would just stop.

And then the screams do stop. I quit shouting and begging. The air is foggy and quiet for a long minute. Behind me, someone whispers.

"Mariam?"

I turn around on my knees, blinking away tears. She stands in front of my eyes, shoulders sagging, face confused at the sight of me. Her frizzy hair sticks up, small mouth in the shape of an O. Her tiny three year old body is standing right in front of me.

I jump onto my feet and sprint to her, tripping on the way. I pull her shoulders to me and crush her in my arms. She doesn't make a sound, but I feel her hot breath on my ear.

As I smooth her hair back, I feel a cut at the top. It leaves my hand wet. Looking, there's a large opening as if someone brought a…axe down at her. I can see dark blood trailing down her shirt and over her eyes. I try to scream, but nothing comes out. Shocked and scared, I shove her away and crawl backwards.

Behind her, a gloved hand stretches out from the darkness and catches her neck. It drags my sister away from me.

"Mariam, wake up. Wake up!"

My eyes snap open. I choke on air and quickly sit up. I rub my eyes, blinking twice to adjust to the lamp on in my room. My blinds are closed, but outside would still be too dim to throw in any light. I look to my right to find Saultan staring at me through his dark brown eyes.

"Mariam…" he says slowly.

"Yes, what's wrong?" I ask, digging my finger in the corner of my left eye to scratch away crust.

"Nothing's wrong. I came in here to wake you up."

I drop my hand in my lap. "What for?" Do we have to get up early to join Dad at one of his functions? Is Mom expecting important visitors?

"*School*, Mariam," Saultan answers. "You need to get ready for *school*."

Right. Duh. There's school today. That makes sense. I must've forgotten to set my alarm last night. I look at the time. And now I'm late.

Saultan's still staring at me.

"Can I help you?" I ask him.

He licks his lips. "Are you okay?"

"Why wouldn't I be?" I ask, but think 'what do you know? Tell me everything!'

"Nightmare. You were having a nightmare."

I look at his face.

"Yeah, I was having a nightmare."

Saultan doesn't seem to be able to move. "Was she-"

"Mariam!"

Islamiat runs into my room. She looks pretty with her short, black hair curled. She's wearing tight, black jeans, the bottom cuffs stuffed into dark brown boots that end six inches below the knee. The sandy, see-through, silk shirt, with a black t-shirt underneath, helps her sweet smile shine. She displays two gold rings and gold earrings with a crystal ball in the middle.

"Your drivers been waiting for ten minutes," she informs me.

I fall out of bed and head to my bathroom. When passing Islamiat, I flip her hair behind her shoulder.

"Who are you looking cute for?" I ask her over my shoulder.

She looks away and smiles, tugging her sleeves down over her hands.

I brush my teeth, throw on some clothes, and fix the braids in my hair. The nanny quickly prepares me scrambled eggs and toast, which I eat in the car with hot chocolate in a thermo.

If I had known school was going to be so horrible today, I would've stayed in bed.

First off, I was late. And then, I tripped while walking up the wet steps, ripping my jeans on the back (at least on the bottom) and getting muck on the front. The bad luck keeps coming. In first period I realized I didn't do my homework, we have an oral report, *and* the class was supposed to bring their text book. I got an F in that period.

What made things worst is how my friends acted. I wanted to scream. Ashley would scoot away if I got more than fifteen inches to her. May would start flinching, hesitate and scamper away. All I wanted to do was explain.

At lunch, I find an empty table at the back of the cafeteria and sit down alone. I push away empty milk cartons and burrito wrappers to give myself some space. I take a small bite into my greasy pizza.

Someone sits in the seat in front of me and smacks their backpack on the room beside them. I look up and blink at the familiar hot, blazing eyes.

"Hm, it's warmer on this side of the cafeteria than the other side," he remarks.

I stare at Dillon. "What are you doing here?"

"I'm hungry. That is why people go to the cafeteria, because they're hungry, right?'

A giggle I couldn't stop falls out of my mouth.

He smiles. "I kicked myself out. Broke up with Nelci. I wanted to sit with a real friend."

(I'm that real friend!)

I turn around in my seat, desperately wanting little Nelci to see Dillon sitting with me. She isn't at the popular table, but Dillon's old friends keep looking back at us as if expecting us to do something extraordinary. Or maybe they're just shocked and secretly crushed that they were replaced with someone like me.

"Where is she?" I asked.

"In the bathroom. Crying," he then adds.

"Because of the breakup?"

"Either that or her wig fell off in class."

I burst out laughing and Dillon joins in. "I'm sorry, but did you just say that Nelci- cheerleader, popular, beautiful Nelci- wears a wig?" I ask, eyes wide.

Dillon's grinning, dimples deep and eyes gleaming. "Yeah. I went camping with her and her family last weekend and her little brother literally burned half her hair off. She basically only has the left side now and the right side hasn't grown back yet. She told me not to tell anyone when we were going out. Well, were not going out now, so I decided to tell the one person who would care."

I laugh a little more. Slowly, my mouth shuts and I remember why I'm alone, what's wrong with me, and that things will get worse soon.

"So, having a bad day?" he asks. His eyes show my worry.

I heave a sigh. "Is it that easy to tell?"

"No, I know you enough to read the expression in your pretty eyes. Say," he searches around, "where's Ashley and May?"

(Whoa, did Dillon just call my eyes pretty?)

"Beats me."

He covers my hands with his. "You want to talk about it?"

Not really. I stare at my pizza.

"Am I allowed to guess?" he said.

I feel myself smile. I nod.

"Let's see…is it volleyball?"

I shrug. There's more.

"So it is volleyball. You didn't make it to tryouts because you had homework?"

I shake my head.

"You were grounded?"

Another shake. He'll never guess correctly.

"Don't tell me it was because of another guy," he begs, smiling like he did when he was ten. The smile is much cuter now.

Dillon's two fingers hold under my chin and lift my face. "Please tell me there isn't another guy."

My mouth opens slightly. Dillon inches his face closer. I do too. The world around me freezes. I close my mouth. My lids fall over my eyes. I feel his breath against my face. Against my lips.

And then the bell rings.

Darn it.

He moves away first. Then I do, but you don't know how much I didn't want to. We both put our backpacks on, I throw away my pizza and Dillon walks me to class. It's a silent walk. So silent that I dared myself to scream at the cute boy walking beside me to do something. To make it better.

Of course, I would never embarrass myself like that. He leaves me at my classroom.

I fail another test. I also accidentally forgot to remind myself to do the homework last night. And as I'm walking out of class, Mr. Ellen stops me. I lean against a wobbly desk as all the students leave for their last class. When the room is vacant except for me and my teacher, I step up to his brown, long desk. His skinny, white fingers trail across the keyboard without looking.

He breaks away from his computer and leans back in his chair. "Your grade is falling, Mariam."

"I've noticed," I say, my face blank.

He connects his hands and places them behind his head. "We need to fix this."

"I'm working on it."

"Maybe we should work together," he suggests.

"Thank you, but I don't need any help."

"You need to trust me."

No way is that going to happen. I stare down at the floor. I shut my eyes.

Size: thin, flat. Color: white. Touch: smooth, weak. Writing:

"Mariam, please come to the office right after class."

A piece of paper blinks into my hand. Specifically, a note from the principle saying I need to see him after class. Pretty clever, right?

"I'm here to help you Mariam, that's why I signed up for this job-"

I stop him and hold up the fake note. "I'm so sorry, but I have to go see the principle."

"Okay, but did you hear *any*thing I just said?" he asks, as he watches me hurry to the door.

"Oh, of course Mr. Ellen," I lie. "I'll try better."

"I don't want you to *try*, I want you to *do*."

"Uh-huh." I leave the room.

I find my locker and hit my head against it, ignoring the passing students in the hallway. The sounds of giggling party girls and shouting jocks seem miles away.

Two of my grades are down to the floor. I feel far away from volleyball and closer to failing this school year.

"Let me see a purse!" Ms. Bell demands.

Size: as big as my head, oval shaped, skinny string attached. Color: black, brown fur on top, silver zipper in the middle. Touch: creamy soft, furry, the zipper is scratchy. Scent: clean, new.

It appears in my hand. I throw it away.

"Sweet pea perfume!" another demand.

Size: small, five inches long, square top. Color: pink and pink, with a curvy, white flower on the cover. Touch: shiny, glass, polished. Scent: strong, luscious, and sweet.

It appears. I throw it away.

"Very good. A pair of jeans!"

Size: size three in juniors, wide at the waist, skinny at the foot. Color: dark blue, yellowish stitches at the sides, a black button under the waist and a silver zipper under that. Touch: smooth fabric, comfortable, square pockets at the front and back. Scent: uh…fabric.

The jeans appear exactly how I imagined it. I throw them away after Ms. Bell gets a good look at them.

She lets my mind rest. "You're a fast thinker," she comments.

"I sort it out," I admit.

She nods at no question. "Impressive."

For twenty minutes, Ms. Bell explains how to create a heart and brain. She tells me animals are easier than humans because human brains are complicated and human hearts need to be extremely strong. I didn't know if she was insulting how good my power is or not.

Creating a heart was actually really easy. That is, if you've seen a real heart in life. Brains are difficult and I had to throw most of my strength into creating it. I made a kitten and a hamster. The hamster came out limping: one leg wasn't as well-made as the other three. The kitten had a bad odor to it, which I did not do on purpose. It was like rotten-egg bad odor.

After I had disposed the animals in my head, the door slowly opens. Islamiat sticks her head in, her eyes searching the room until she finds us.

"Mom said she'd like it if you ate dinner with the family," she informs me.

"I see I'm being kicked out," Ms. Bell mummers.

"Sorry," I apologize.

"It's alright. You go eat with your family. I'll let myself out," she pats my shoulder as she passes me and Islamiat and goes out the door.

I leave the room minutes later, my younger sister right behind me.

"How can you study without any books or paper?" she asks.

"Don't worry about it," I snap.

"Just wondering," she grumbles.

We both step into the kitchen and take our seats. Dad and mom are the head of the table. Mom's on my left and Islamiat is on my right. Jamui's across from me with Saultan to his left. We're all quiet. I take a sip of my water.

Dad's phone rings. He slips it out of his pocket and checks the caller. The person isn't important. Dad rejects the caller and puts the phone away, bringing up his hand to rub the part between his brown eyes.

Dad's a child custody lawyer. Meaning, when parent's divorce, he makes sure the child, or children, is given to the correct parent. I've seen lots of interesting couples. A business man with a drug addict woman. The father believes his ex-wife won't protect their daughter and wants full custody. Then there's the sweet lady with the criminal boyfriend wanting to keep the unlucky twins. It's always obvious who the child should go to, but the wrong parent throws in so many problems against the other. It's a stressful job, you can tell just by looking into my father's eyes. But he loves his work, and grins each time the child is going home to sleep in the right house.

Right now he smiles at me as I realize I'm staring.

Our chef (he comes to prepare our dinner three times a week) walks up from behind me and sets my dishes of salad, rice, corn, and chicken on the table in front of me. He sets down a glass of water beside me. The chef places the same plates in front of the rest of my family. There's a glass of water for everyone. The chef leaves once all the food, silverware, and napkins are placed properly.

We pray, and then eat.

My dad grabs the pepper and sprinkles some onto his salad. "How's school Islamiat?"

"Good," she answers plainly.

"And you, Mariam?"

I nod. "Okay."

"What about you, Saultan?" Dad asks.

Immediately, a smile spreads across his face. "Awesome. We had a sub for first period but the sub took forever to get to school, so we were left outside to do whatever. Then there was a fire drill in third period so we missed half an hour of class. There was a fight at lunch and we watched a movie in my last two periods," he grins, peeling meat off the bone with his fingers.

"So you didn't learn anything today?" Dad questions.

Saultan thinks for a second. "Nope."

Dad smiles at his son's shinning face.

Jamui takes a bite of his rice, his eyes averting ours. I stare at him.

"How's tutoring going, Mariam?" my mom asks.

"Yeah Mariam, how's the tutoring?" Islamiat asks, very suspicious. "I mean, considering you guys don't use anything."

I ignore her and Mom. I stare only at Jamui. I know he feels my gaze.

"What does she mean by that?" Mom says to me.

I don't answer. I keep staring.

"Mariam, your mothers talking to you. Answer her," dad demands.

"Why not ask *Jamui* how his day's been?"

Everyone looks at me after the words leave my mouth. I catch Jamui twitch. My dad stiffens and my mom looks at her hands. But I still stare.

"So, how was your day, Jamui?" I ask, my voice slowly rising.

He doesn't speak. Eyes only on his food.

"Mariam, don't-" Dad warns.

"Why won't you speak, huh?" I ask, glaring. "How can you not speak for over three months to your own family? What is your problem? She's *dead* Jamui- get over it!" I shout.

Mom and Islamiat gasps. Saultan closes his eyes. My dad looks around, as if searching for the button to switch me off.

And finally, he looks up. We make eye contact. And I watch as a tear falls down his cheek.

I screech my chair back, throwing my spoon onto my plate. I run up the stairs and slam my door shut behind me.

I feel like stabbing myself. What kind of sister am I?

CHAPTER 11

After school, Ms. Bell waits patiently in the library as I pace around in my room, my phone pressed roughly to my ear. For the third time, I get the answering machine.

"Ashley, please pick up," I beg. "How many times do you need me to say sorry? Please call me back."

I hang up. Five minutes later, I punch her number again. And, thank the Lord, she actually picks up this time. With an attitude.

"What?"

I ignore her tone even though I so want to give it right back to her. "You picked up."

"Only way to make you stop calling," she mutters.

I sigh. "I'm sorry."

She doesn't speak.

"Ashley, are you still there?"

"Yeah."

"Did you hear me?"

"Yeah."

I sigh again, beginning to get frustrated. "How many times do you need me to say it?"

"Until you say it to my face," she replies roughly.

"When?" I ask, quietly as if this is all a secret.

"Today. Right now," she answers.

I think of Ms. Bell waiting in the library for me. "I-I can't." My eyes are squeezed shut to anticipate her anger.

"Wow, why am I not surprised?"

"Ashley, I'm sorry-"

"Talk to you later, Mariam."

"No!" I shout into the phone.

But she already hung up.

"Did you apologize?" Ms. Bell asks, sounding worried. I kind of hope she is worried. I like knowing someone's worried for me.

"More times than I can remember," I say.

"Then what happened?"

"She wants me to say it to her face. Right now."

Ms. Bell sighs and sits on the table next to me in the library. Causally, she wraps her arm around my back, allowing my head to fall onto her shoulder. She rubs my shoulder with her hand, comforting me. I used to tense up at her touch and step away. Now her hands on me feel almost as good as when my mom does it. I close my eyes so that tears don't fall out.

"It's okay," she doesn't stop rubbing my shoulder as she talks. "True friends never leave. No matter what they say, or what they do, they're still going to be there for you. They will always be there for you."

I snort. "My friends can't stand it when I'm near them."

Ms. Bell tugs on my braids. "They'll come around. They're not mad at how you acted. They're mad that they missed you so much."

My eyebrows scrunch up. "No, I think Ashley is pretty mad I made her look stupid when she arrived at the party and I wasn't there with the preparations. All the guests were outside, freezing their butts off. They blamed it all on her and she probably felt like she ruined May's birthday when it was my entire fault really."

"How long have you guys been friends?" Ms. Bell suddenly asks.

I know the answer immediately. “Second grade.”

Ms. Bell nods. “She’ll get over it.”

I hope so, I thought.

She steps away from the table and stands in front of me. “Today’s lesson needs lots of your brains attention. This time, we’re going to create multiple things. The more you concentrate on the creations you make, the better they’ll stay in one piece.”

“Okay,” I close my eyes.

“A blue and green nail polish,” she says.

Size: square bottle, glass, blue liquid. Touch: smooth, wet. Smell: strong.

I feel a smooth, short glass bottle form in my hand. Separating my brain to think on two different things, I rethink the nail polish. But this time, I make sure the liquid is green. I feel the same glass bottle appear in my other hand. I open my eyes.

My right hand holds a perfect, glassy bottle of blue nail polish. My left hand holds the same perfect, glassy bottle, but instead of blue, green.

“Set it on the table,” she instructs.

I do as she said.

“Two green apples.”

I think of the apple the same way I thought about it on the first lesson I had. Once I have one, green and soft, I think it over again. I set the two apples on the table next to the blue and green nail polish.

“Two candy canes,” Ms. Bell orders.

Size: six inches long, top loops downward, a little fatter than a pencil. Color: red, white, red, white. Touch: soft, hard, crumples on corners, sticky when wet. Smell and taste: peppermint.

I think it once more.

As I’m laying the two candy canes on the table, the nail polishes blink away with a light. Darn it.

“Don’t forget the others,” Ms. Bell reminds me. A little too late now.

I thought about whining that I didn’t, but I was guilty.

I try again.

And again.

And again.

"Until you get it right," says Ms. Bell.

Until you get it right, I mock her in my head.

Having to think it over and over, and having it disappear on me even when I just think of something else real quick, doesn't make my insides try to kill me. No. This time, it just gives me an extreme headache and makes me want to strangle Miss Bell.

"Try one more time?" my tutor suggests.

I shake my head and drop it in my hands.

"Here, take some of this."

I force my head up as Ms. Bell comes over with the same blue liquid that seems to be saving my life more than I can. I open my mouth and Ms. Bell tosses some down my throat. My headache skips away.

"Go get some rest," she gives me another order. But I like this one. "And try to practice on today's lesson."

Two minutes later, I step into my room, shut my door, and purposely fall on my bed, face first. I squeeze my eyes shut. I'm hardly able to pump four more heartbeats before I hear a loud, terrified scream coming from across the hall. Suddenly, I'm fully awake and running out of my room. I race towards Saultan's room, the scream seeming to echo through the air.

I smash open his door. Lying on his bed, his face stuffed into his pillow, Saultan whines and pleads. Pleads someone to stop doing something. I'm afraid to know what he wants it to stop doing.

I sit on his bed and push him into my arms. I lift his head off his pillow and let it fall against my stomach. Quickly, Saultan's tears start to drench my shirt. His pillow already has a wet spot the size of a golf ball. Saultan wraps his skinny arms around my body and squeezes me hard, like he's making sure I'm really here.

Islamiat runs into the room. The nanny stops behind her and scoots inside.

"What happened?" she asks, looking at Saultan who is now sniffing up all his snot like a three year old.

"Nothing, he just had a bad dream. It's okay," I assure her.

"O-okay," the nanny sighs, gives my brother one more look over, and leaves the room.

Islamiat stands in her spot as if she's not sure she believed me at all. I look down at Saultan and pat his head.

"You want to talk about it?" I ask him.

He squeezes me tighter. Islamiat slowly sits down on the edge of his bed.

"I was tired, s-so I went to sleep," he stutters, his face still pressed to my stomach. "But then I had a scary dream."

You're probably wondering how a twelve year old going to seventh grade next year is crying to his older sister about a bad dream. I'm wondering that too.

"It's okay, Saultan," I calm him down. "Everyone gets bad dreams once in a while."

"About our baby sister?"

I stop moving and my eyes widen. I look at Islamiat, but she's staring at Saultan. Not staring, but glaring at him with her light brown eyes.

"It was back when I was tickling her and she was laughing and smiling. B-but I don't know what happened. I don't know what I did. But she starts to choke and she doesn't stop," he embraces me so tight I have trouble breathing. I feel paralyzed; I can't move to let him loosen his grip. "She kept choking and choking. And when she does stop, she doesn't move. Because she's dead!" Saultan starts to cry, his trembling body shaking me along with him. "I killed her. I killed my baby sister!"

I don't move. He keeps crying. Islamiat stares into space. For two minutes straight, we stay like that. The movement of Saultan switching into a sitting position unfreezes me. I stare at him as he wipes more snot off from under his nose and blinks down at his jeans.

"Stop crying like a baby."

I look up at Islamiat, the one who spoke the words. She sneers at Saultan.

"Not everything's about you Saultan. You cry all the time! Your twelve years old, it's about time you start acting your age!" she yells at him.

I smack my sister on the arm to get her to stop.

I'm not very surprised by her attitude. She's always been a little drama queen. But not only that. She loves attention; been like that forever. It's very annoying but I've gotten so used to it that I'm surprised when *she's* quiet to let the other person brag. But right now she's not being a drama queen or bragging about a new shirt, or even being a mean sister. She's not mad at her crying sibling. She's mad at the dead one that had taken away all her attention when she was alive.

"Shut up!" Saultan shouts at her, but his voice sounded so weak that it wouldn't scare a fly.

"You little baby!" she teases. "I hope you go back to sleep and kill her again."

"Islamiat, what is wrong with you!" I scream and push her off the bed. "Get out of here."

"Oh my gosh!" she roars at the ceiling. "Does no one care for me?"

"Not with that attitude," I say.

She stomps out of the room and slams her bedroom door in frustration and hatred.

Saultan clutches my arm. "I don't mean to kill her, Mariam. I swear. I can't stop what I dream."

I stare at his wet, brown eyes.

I remember when Ms. Bell asked me to see how Saultan was doing, advising that I go talk to him to see how he feels. I tried to be funny and suggested we switch and she talk to him herself. It doesn't sound very funny anymore. Why would I think that I'm the only one that can't let go?

I look down at Saultan, finally noticing the bumps under his eyes, the way his shoulders sag, and the look he gives me. He likes to laugh, he loves to smile. Right now, he's doing neither of those things and I'm stuck wondering where my real brother was abducted to.

I sigh and pat his arm. "It's okay, it was just a nightmare," I tell him.

"But its goanna come back. I have one every night. In my dreams, I kill her."

That night, I was so restless that my eyes wouldn't stay shut longer than a minute. Saultan slept like a baby beside me, his hand attached to my arm. When I heard him snore, I knew he hadn't had a long, nice sleep in a while. Hopefully not as long as three months.

Irritated that I'm so wide awake, I slide my arm out of Saultan's hold. I pull my feet out from under my dark blue covers and set them on the carpet. I push my feet into my slippers, grab my robe out of my closet, and pull it on. Quietly, I creep out of my room and down the stairs.

I walk down the two hardwood steps. I enter the kitchen, look to the side, and stop.

Jamui stuffs the last piece of cookie in his mouth and drinks down the last bit of milk in his cup. He looks stiff leaning against the table. I didn't stop because I didn't want to be seen, because I knew he heard me, but because I'm scared of what would come if I do step in the kitchen. Like I said, I hate saying sorry.

But I watch him ignore me as I grab a glass out of the cabinet and fill it with ice cold water. I take a sip. And another. But it doesn't make me feel any different and definitely not any better. Just as I set the cup in the sink, I hear a voice I had forgotten.

"It's too hard for me to forget her."

I stare and stare. What? I can't believe this.

"Every part of this house reminds me of her," he continues. "To forget her, is to forget life."

"I never said to forget her," I say, still completely shocked, my mouth trembles when I speak. "When she died, she took your voice with her. A voice I missed."

Jamui looks up in my eyes. "I was mourning."

I lay a hard gaze on him. "You mourn on her funeral. You remember the great moments every other day. You don't mourn the rest of your life."

He blinks. "I'm sorry."

I shake my head. "Shouldn't I be the one saying that?"

And then he shakes his head. "No. Y-you were there. If you remember or not, your eyes saw everything happen."

No, I remember it all.

"What are you talking about?" I ask. But I know exactly what he's talking about.

"When he took her. Not just away from your arms but away from this world."

And lots more, I think. He gave me a power I don't want and don't need. Gave Islamiat the attention she prayed for. Took away Saultan's good dreams and Jamui's voice. But Jamui got his voice back. I'm working on Saultan's dreams, and Islamait will never change. Maybe she should try out for acting, so that the audience would give her the attention she desires. And me? I guess I have to die or cut open my head to lose my gift.

"You should get up stairs before Saultan's nightmare comes," Jamui says. He goes to the sink and places his cup and plate inside it.

My eyebrows scrunch together. "You know about that?"

He shrugs like old Jamui does. "I hear him crying in his room almost every night."

"Oh, right," I say. I look down at my hands.

We're both quiet.

"Mariam...do you want to know her name?" asks Jamui.

Do I? I bet you're surprised that I still can't remember what her name was. Not the first letter and not if it's short or long or girly or if it comes off smooth on the tongue or if you need a certain accent to say it.

When I had woken up from after getting hit by the car and my head stitched closed, I lost lots of names. I remember Mom's,

Dad's, Dillon's, Jamui's, Islamiat's, and Saultan's. It took me a while to get May's and Ashley's right. Everyone else's we're gone, though their face and memories we're familiar. I also forgot numbers to phones and the alarm system and even what two digits our mailbox was.

Mom helped me fill in everyone else's name. And then when she brought up our baby sister, I stopped her. Told her that I wanted to figure it out by myself. She understood, but I had no idea it would be this hard and take this long.

And I feel myself nod, because I actually do want to know my baby sisters name. Why? I have no idea. Something's telling me that I'm going to need to know her name if I'm going to survive the next few days. And I want my big brother to be the one to tell me.

"Erika."

I look up into Jamui's face, confused.

"Our baby sister. Her name was Erika."

CHAPTER 12

Right after school on Wednesday, my driver is replaced by Shelly and her yellow beetle. Once I notice her behind the wheel, I climb in without a word. The inside of her car smelt like peppermint and a little bit like strawberries. Maybe that was the perfume she's wearing today or what she put in her mouth just a moment ago. Her hair is down, the curls touching her lower back. With the sun hiding behind two huge clouds, the golden brown highlights seem to almost blend in with her natural black hair. She has on only light makeup today: faint eyeliner and pale, pink lip gloss.

She takes me to her office. The whole ride, we never open our mouth to conversant. I didn't know what to say to her. I was afraid she'd scream at me, but I don't know why. She couldn't possibly still be mad about Malcolm.

She shuts the door to her office and moves to her computer. I stand in the middle of the room. She punches her secret code in with the keyboard and the bookshelf slides to the right. I follow her to the opposite side of the door, the lab where procedures are created, experiments are tested, and machines formed objects.

The medicine, smoke, and animal smell is still in the air. My tennis shoes still squeak on the floor too. Wind keeps blowing from the huge fans and the machines at every side cruise on with their loud noise. The annoying things in your life never change.

A few scientists are around working on projects. They're oblivious to us as we work our way to the back of the lab. Once we pass the caged animals, Shelly and I can hear voices up ahead. It sounds like two men arguing.

Dr. Jeff is sitting in his chair in front of his computer. Or he was until he leaped out of his seat, pulling a device out of Malcolm's hands, begging him to stop touching everything. He tells him he would probably be better off waiting in Shelly's office, adding that he's not supposed to be in here anyways. And judging by the way Shelly's face turns red and her eyes burn with hate, there was no plan on seeing each other today.

"Malcolm, *please*, go find a seat in her office," Dr. Jeff pleads.

"What's there to hide, huh?" the FBI agent questions the doctor. He picks up a scalpel, twirling it in his fingers. "Is there something you should tell me?"

"What the hell are you doing here?"

Malcolm turns around at Shelly's stiff voice. Dr. Jeff looks up. He steps away from Malcolm at the sight of the agent's angry stance. Malcolm only smiles and crosses his arms.

"Why do you have a lab hiding behind your wall, darling?" he asks. His eyes browse on me for a moment.

"Why do you care?" Shelly says.

"Does everyone else in this building know this is here?"

"Of course."

Malcolm lifts his chin. "And the police? The FBI?"

"Yes."

Dr. Jeff squints at the lie.

"Then why don't I know about this place?" Malcolm asked.

"Why are you here?" Shelly dismisses his question.

"Oh you know, just curious as to what you have been doing lately."

"Which is none of your business. Now leave, you stupid idiot."

Malcolm looks sideways at Dr. Jeff. "Isn't she sweet?"

"The sweetest," Dr. Jeff answers.

"I got your text."

Shelly and I turn around at the voice.

Ms. Bell's wearing a brown coat with the collar up. It must've started to drizzle or snow once we got here because her hair is wet and her eyeliner looks smeared. She has on a white shirt with blue jeans and tall, black boots. She's holding a small purse in her hand, lazily, as if it's too heavy. She looks tired all over.

"Ah, yes, so you did. Um," Shelly looks back at Malcolm, who's obviously not going anywhere anytime soon. "About that, what I was planning on telling you today can just be told over the phone."

Ms. Bell's eyebrows scrunch together. "But you said it's confidential-"

"Please," Malcolm speaks up with his eyes on Shelly, "don't let my presence ruin your guy's plan. Just pretend I'm not even here."

Shelly snorts and my tutor's eyebrows slide even closer together. Dr. Jeff pushes his glasses up his nose.

"Doctor, a word," commands Shelly.

Dr. Jeff moves from behind his desk and stands before Shelly. Malcolm stays in his spot, taking over the doctor's chair and slapping the scalpel against his leg for a beat. Ms. Bell steps closer to us and the three adults huddle in a circle. Though I'm not welcomed inside, I can hear them perfectly fine.

"He can't be here," said Shelly. "How did he even get in?" Moment of silence while I'm sure they stare accusingly at Dr. Jeff.

"What was I supposed to do?" he asks. "He caught me coming in. I couldn't just tell him that the sliding bookshelf is his imagination."

"What's wrong with explaining what's really going on?" Ms. Bell wonders.

"What's wrong?" Shelly repeats. "What's wrong is that there are only four people who know, that knowing this information can put you in danger, and that Malcolm doesn't know how to keep his big mouth shut."

"Well," Dr. Jeff crosses his arms, "those are good reasons. But he's no leaving."

The three of them look over at him. He stopped tapping his leg with the scalpel, and instead, is using it to clean his fingernails. His feet are on the desk, leaning back in his chair, with his gun peeking out from around his waist and under his coat. The adults switch back to their conversation and it's only me who keeps my eyes on the FBI agent.

I see him different from the way Shelly described him. I can't imagine him screaming in her face to desperately win an argument, or cheating behind her back to make her feel sorry. I see a man pulling a trigger to save her life and holding her face in his hands to make sure she's alright. He cares. I know he does. And deep down, so does Shelly.

Take care of Shelly for me. She doesn't have anybody else.

Malcolm sees me watching him and winks at me with his blue eye.

"You should tell us all you can with him listening," I hear from Ms. Bell.

"Good idea," Dr. Jeff agrees.

They break apart. Malcolm gets more comfortable in the chair and Ms. Bell leans against the desk. Dr. Jeff pushes his glasses further up his nose, eyeing Malcolm's feet by his work. Shelly, with her arms crossed and hair trembling from the incessant fans, stands before us with confident eyes.

> "I brought us together today," she says, pausing to glare at Malcolm's innocent smile, "to announce that Ike Henderson has murdered again."
>
> "Yes, we know," said Ms. Bell. "A Suzette-"
>
> "Not her. A different child. A boy."
>
> Malcolm's feet drop from the desk. "When did this happen?"

"Last night at eleven forty-three. Eight years old. His throat was slit in bed. Painless and messy."

"Painless?" I say, feeling my own throat and trying to swallow.

"He was asleep."

"Dying in your sleep is as painless as it's going to get," adds Dr. Jeff.

Malcolm leans forward, looking a little distraught. "Slow down. How come the FBI doesn't know about this?"

"Because Malcolm, we were able to stop the FBI's big fat nose from sticking into our business," Shelly explains, not trying to soften her words.

Malcolm groans. "I need to notify them." He reaches for his cellphone in his pocket.

"Go ahead. Notify them all you want. The body is gone. The bed sheets and mattress have been destroyed and the room sprayed. There's nothing left to look for."

Malcolm stares at her like he just realized that she's told a thousand lies to him. "Why?"

"Because you guys need to back down. This isn't your problem," Shelly said.

"How many times do I need to tell you? We're on the same side."

"I'm hoping that's the last time."

"Guys, back to the problem," Dr. Jeff interrupts their annoying spat.

The two ex's stare at each other a little longer and then Shelly looks away.

"The crime scene," she begins, "is 102 miles away. Suzette Morales house is forty miles away and the child before her was twenty one miles away."

"How is this important?" Malcolm asks.

"Don't you see? The murders are moving farther and farther away from us."

"Is that good?" I ask.

"Well, good and bad. The good news is the people around here are safe. The bad news: he's moving to the next city."

"How do you know that for sure?" questions Malcolm.

"I don't know that *for sure*. It's just a hunch, but it's a pretty darn good one. He killed the one's he wanted in this city, and now he's going off to the next one."

It's quiet for a moment as Shelly's words sink in.

"What's the plan?" asks Ms. Bell.

"We take action before he gets too far. We stick to *our* plan," Shelly said, throwing a sideways glance at me. "I informed the police about the distance miles and they said they'll look into it. But that's the problem. There's nothing to look *into* about Ike Henderson."

"You're right," Malcolm agrees. "This guy has no car, no house, and no money. He has no friends or living relatives and no one we've ever questioned has ever seen his face."

I look down at the floor. I've seen his face perfectly fine, every dent and every wrinkle.

Malcolm keeps going. "He doesn't leave obvious clues like other murderers do just to play with us. He kills and then goes on to the next one." He rubs his face. "We're basically trying to find a red ant on a football field."

"I'm guessing you didn't catch any answers on that piece from his jeans that you stole from me," Shelly assumes.

"Just dirt and some more dirt."

Ms. Bell sighs. "This is hopeless."

"Have a little faith," Malcolm says, but he looks too tired to smile.

"This guy is murdering kids out there and the police aren't running after him."

"The police are tired," Shelly explains. "They're done chasing. They're just going to wait until he messes up."

"They can't do that. This man killed my nephew."

"I know and I'm sorry, but they don't know what else to do."

"Why can't we just trap him?" I blurt.

Malcolm squints at me. "How?"

"Discover his next target and be there to catch him," I said. With everyone's eyes on me, it feels like I'm about to present a project to the class and one screw up and there'll be a wave of laughter.

"It'll be impossible to know who he'll go after next," Dr. Jeff said, stuffing his large hands in his lab pockets.

"But the miles," I continue. "If he actually is moving farther away in the same direction, then we'll have a chance at who will be next. Twenty cops hiding around the kid and when he appears, he'll be trapped."

I can see it now. Ike Henderson, my baby sister's murderer, falling to the ground with twenty bullets in his chest.

"That's too easy," Shelly shakes her head. "That won't be enough."

"I don't know," Malcolm disagrees with her. "Sounds pretty good to me. Twenty officers with twenty guns trained on his head. It does sound too easy. For *us*."

Another shake from Shelly. "No. He'll see it coming. And even if he doesn't, he's smart enough to find a way to get out before we'll be able to touch him."

Malcolm stands, staring at Shelly. "What are you talking about? This murderer might be a little more intelligent but he's just like any other. He can't fly and he can't block bullets. Right?"

Malcolm looks at each of us in the face, and when his eyes hit mine, I look away before he can see the truth in my expression. I bite my lip, hoping I know how to lie without saying a word.

The FBI agent sighs. "You guys are hiding something really important."

He turns back to Shelly.

"Keeping secrets will get officers killed out there if they don't know what they're up against. Is that what you want Shelly? To put your partners in jeopardy?"

She doesn't say anything.

Malcolm slides past Dr. Jeff and Ms. Bell. "Do as you guys please. If you don't want the FBI in your way, then we'll go a different direction. An agent, scientist, therapist, and a high school girl. Yeah, that's definitely a team to be afraid of."

Malcolm leaves us, his shoes slapping against the tile as he rushes to the front of the lab. Shelly's staring down at her hands and I wonder what she's thinking. Malcolm's words must be making her contemplate over a lot of things, but is that good or bad? What if this secret is better to keep than to share?

I feel a hand on my arm and I turn to see Dr. Jeff.

"Let me take a look at you."

I let him check my eyes, my mouth, and my hands. His fingers are soft, lifting my chin up higher and pressing his thumb in my palm. His glasses look cloudy and he's expressionless but I can almost see his thoughts running through his brain behind his crystal blue eyes.

In the corner of the room, I can hear Ms. Bell and Shelly talking. Maybe they're discussing Ike's expanding distance and maybe they're discussing the secret only four people know. Or maybe they're talking about me.

I watch Dr. Jeff as he scans my left palm.

"What do you think about all of this?" I ask.

"What part?" he said. He bends my middle finger back. It cracks from the pressure.

"What Malcolm said. Keeping the secret away from other people," I remind him.

Dr. Jeff licks his lips. "Secrets are meant to be kept to yourself."

"So…you agree with Shelly?"

"I don't agree or disagree."

I roll my eyes and take my hand back. "Thanks, that helps a lot."

Dr. Jeff smiles to himself.

"I think she should tell him. I know he can keep a secret."

"To tell half the secret you must tell all," he said.

“What does that mean?”

“You my dear. To say Ike Henderson is a Constitutor, she needs to say that you are too. Maybe she doesn’t care if Malcolm knows that Ike has the power to create anything. But I’m sure she cares if he knows that *you* can too.”

“But no one would care about me.”

Dr. Jeff raises his eyebrows at me. “No one would care? Dear, you’d be the most important person in the world.”

Important person in the world.

Dr. Jeff moves in front of his computer and I look towards Ms. Bell and Shelly. They’re arguing now and they seem to keep gazing at me.

‘Our plan’ Shelly had said.

What the hell is *our* plan?

CHAPTER 13

The moment I wake up, I notice everyone's gone, including the nanny. My room is cold and my pillow is wet on the corner. I must've cried when I dreamt of Ike Henderson wasting my sister's blood. It was on the floor and walls and in his hands. No, not his hands but mine.

Once I get out of bed, I brush my teeth, comb my hair, dress, and search the fridge. Yes, there's food, lots of it. Only I can't cook. I make scrambled eggs look like bird poop. I shut the fridge.

The doorbell rings and I go to answer it. Swinging the door open, Ms. Bell smiles at me with the wind blowing at her hair.

"Thank God, you're awake," she says. "I thought I was going to have to drag you out of bed."

"Why is there practice today?" I ask, not letting her in.

"There's practice every day. Now let me in, it's freezing."

I step aside, frowning, and let her in. I shut the door. Ms. Bell throws of her brown coat and tosses it on the chair beside the door like she's done so often. Same coat. Same chair.

She looks around and takes a second to listen. "No one home?"

"No."

"No reason to give an attitude."

I sigh. And I am not about to say sorry. "There shouldn't be practice today. It's Saturday. Saturday means relaxing."

"It says that in the dictionary?" asks Ms. Bell.

I roll my eyes. "That's not what I mean. Everyone knows that you relax on Saturday. You throw on sweats, eat ice cream, and maybe watch a drama movie. You just stay home and hang loose."

"Where's the rest of your family while you 'hang loose'?"

I shrug. "Don't know. Maybe they're getting donuts to make relaxing a lot better."

Ms. Bell rolls her eyes exactly like I did. "Mariam, this is important and we have a lot of work to do. We're behind because I was sick all week."

How is that my fault?

I cross my arms. "I am not doing it today."

"And who's going to stop me?" she ask, eyebrows rose.

I go call Agent Clark.

"What is this all about, Miss Wilson?"

I shrug at Shelly's question. "I don't want to do a lesson today."

I sit down on a bench beside the front door. Shelly sits beside me and Ms. Bell leans her back against the staircase, looking disappointed that I actually brought Shelly all the way to my house.

"There's no time to be stalling a practice. You're already behind," said Shelly.

"I'm not doing it."

"Miss Wilson-"

"No!" I shout, threatening to start a tantrum- even though I sort of have. "I'm through! I've almost died twice. I've thrown up and cried blood. I've lost my two best friends and I'm failing just about every class. And I've recently noticed that my little brother gets nightmares each night about our baby sister. You go tell Ike Henderson that I am *not* a threat to him!" I yell.

Finished with my speech, I jump off the bench and run down the steps into the kitchen. I hear their four feet walking in behind me.

"And what do you think will happen to those other kids?" Shelly asks, her voice curious.

I slowly turn around. "What do you mean?"

"You haven't been watching the news?"

Confused, I wait impatiently as she slides two doors away on the wall, revealing the flat screen T.V. I step into the family room and stand beside Shelly. She turns it on and flips to a different channel. She turns up the volume for us to listen to the newscaster.

Beside the blond newscaster, is a picture of a cute, little boy around the age of seven. His name is Davy.

"Only two hours ago his parents found him in his room dead," the newscaster explains, paper in her painted hand and shoulders up high. "His wrists were slit and he had bled to death. The parents know this is not a suicide and no one else thinks it is. There have been many reports of children being murdered rapidly under the age of thirteen. The police are still doing their best to find the people killing innocent children. Parents are hiding their children in their houses after school hours. No one knows who they're after now. But we do know that the police need to find these people before they ruin another life. Davy-"

Shelly shuts off the T.V. and closes it up. "Disappointingly, this one got out. I was at his home when you called me to come over. What do you think of that?"

I shrug like I really don't care. "I think it's pretty funny that they believe there's more than one guy."

"Really? Did you think it was pretty funny when they thought more than one guy helped kill your sister?"

My face freezes. I don't speak or look at her.

"Yeah, I didn't think so.

"So many kids are born like this, Miss Wilson," she says. "So many kids are born like this every year. Ike Henderson won't stop until they're all dead, because he is so determined to be the only one left. But nothing is going to stop them from being born. So he won't stop killing. I'm sorry we're stacking this all on you," she tells me. "But right now it's not *about* you. It's about all those other kids out there right now, not knowing they're going to die because of the way they were born. Like your sister."

I finally look up at her. Not to give her a glare. To see if there's actually sympathy in her eyes. There is.

"You're the only hope we have, Miss Wilson. Without you, we might as well wait until Ike Henderson kills himself. Which is going to be years from now.

"Ms. Bell, why don't you go home. I'll take care of her," Shelly said.

"Are you sure?" Ms. Bell asks.

"Yes. Thank you."

Ms. Bell walks out of the room and leaves the house. My stomach loudly complains. Shelly looks up when she hears it.

"You didn't eat?"

I shake my head. "I don't know how to cook anything except cereal and toast."

"I'm surprised with this big kitchen," she mumbles under her breath.

She walks over to the fridge and grabs some eggs out of it. She snatches the English muffins from the shelves on the door and closes the fridge. She looks up and sees me standing in the same spot.

"Aren't you going to help?" she raises her eyebrows at me.

Twenty minutes later, we both have on flower-patterned aprons on, the ingredients scattered on the table, skillet on the stove and heating up, and the oven is on, cooking the English muffins. Today's goal: make Eggs Benedict.

I grease the skillet and fill half of it with water. I wait for bubbling to grow and alert Shelly. She carefully cracks two eggs into the heated, bubbly skillet, making sure to give them their own room. As we wait five minutes, Shelly instructs me on making Hollandaise Sauce.

Shelly sets out butter, three egg yolks beaten, lemon juice, salt, and white pepper. I cut the butter into thirds. Shelly had shut off the stove after the whites of the eggs were completely done and the yolks begin to thicken. She sets the lid over the eggs to keep them warm.

I put a pot on the stove. I combine the three egg yolks, one tablespoon of lemon juice and water. I stir it rapidly with a whisk, waiting for the sauce to harden. Shelly adds the butter, one at a time, as I whisk. She then sprinkles in some salt and white pepper, offering it a taste. I'm surprised we even have each of these ingredients. I whisk for two more minutes until I'm sure it's thick enough.

The oven beeps and Shelly takes the two English muffins out. With speed, she puts eight pieces of bacon on a separate skillet, bringing the heat up high to make them cook faster.

After they're done, I watch Shelly place four pieces of bacon in each of our muffins. She uses a spatula to scoop up one egg and the other and set it on top of the muffin. Then she slowly pours the Hollandaise Sauce over the egg, until only the side of the egg is poking out, giving you room to grab it without getting your fingers covered with yellow sauce.

We sit down at the table and I take my first bite. It's delicious.

"It's great. Who knew you could cook like this," I said.

"I try my best," Shelly says and smiles.

The roar of children running past me and screaming on rides fills my ears with joy. I didn't know how good it felt to be able to know that someone is having a good time. Even if it makes me a little bit jealous.

After the tastiest breakfast I've ever had, Shelly brought me to the fair. She said it's a gift for cooperating with Ms. Bell.

Shoulder to shoulder, we walk past small, kiddy rides where the five year olds think they're in Heaven. Shelly buys us both a smoothie and we head over to the large Ferris wheel.

We stand in line for what seems like hours. Between the hours, we both finish our drinks and throw them in the trash. Finally, we're let on. I get in after Shelly. The ticket guy closes the gate that holds us in the seat and locks it. He pushes a glowing green button, and we go up. I lean back as Shelly leans her elbow against the bar in front of us. We have a view that looks out over everyone. The weather is actually great today. The sun is wide awake, shoving away the clouds that always keep it behind.

"How old is your son?" I ask, curious.

She smiles some as if talking about her child is her favorite subject. "He'll be nine in January."

"Oh," I say. I sit in my seat, not sure what to say next is appropriate. I ask anyway. "When you didn't know Ike Henderson was murdering kids because they carry the same power as him, were you scared for your son?" I ask, my voice dropping to a whisper.

Shelly lowers her voice also. "I'm scared for him either way. Ike Henderson killed more children than any murderer I've ever investigated. But there are others still. Others that are emotionless and dangerous just like him. He's not the only one, just the most wanted," she clarifies.

The most wanted. I sigh to myself and lean back.

"He's getting impatient," Shelly suddenly says.

"How do you know?"

"He killed two boys in one week. And Suzette Morales was just last Saturday. He usually takes a one week break before he murders another child. But it feels like he's rushing through them real quick."

"Maybe you guys are one step behind him and he wants to hurry up and get out of the city like you said he would. Maybe he's scared," I suggest.

Shelly laughs. "Scared? He's the murderer, not us. No. Either he has a plan up his sleeve or he thinks we do."

"Do you?" I ask. She turns to look at me, her mouth partway open. In her eyes, I can see the hesitation.

As she's about to answer, I hear a commotion down below. The ticket guy is shouting. We both look over the edge to see what's going on. My heart goes just a little faster.

A tall man pushes the ticket guy out of the way. Two young, blond girls scream as the man pulls them out of their seat once their cart lands. He shoves the ticket guy to the floor and stabs the green button with his finger. The cart starts flowing upward, as our moves higher into the air. Before it flies out of reach, the guy jumps inside the empty cart and slams the gate shut, his black coat flapping in the air.

"Well, someone really wants a ride," Shelly chuckles.

But I'm not sure he's on for the ride.

The man searches around, checking each cart. His eyes, eyes darker and colder than a cave, lock on mine. With his black, long hair sweeping up when the wind plays with it, he watches me, squints at me. And smiles.

I choke on air and look away. I lean back; lean back as far as I can go. My heart is pumping so fast and it feels like I can't breathe. I feel like I'm about to die like when I screw with my power the wrong way.

Ike Henderson is here.

I start shaking uncontrollably.

Shelly holds my shoulders. "Miss Wilson, what's wrong?"

I push her hands off of me and search for a way to get down safely. Except there is no safe place- we're over thirty-five feet in the air.

"What's wrong?" Shelly asks again.

"We have to get down. Now," I add, frightened. "He's here. Ike Henderson's here."

Immediately, Shelly's face shows me she understands. We hear a woman scream below us. We both lean over the edge again to look down. Ike Henderson, my sister's murderer, reaches for the cart lifting over him. The woman cries out as his feet swing out of his own cart and heaves his body into hers. She backs herself to the side as he stands up right. She hides her face with her purse but he barely gives her a glance as he reaches for the next cart above, which holds a skater and his girlfriend. They look around panicky at the oncoming murderer. The cart right below us. I have to do something.

I close my eyes and concentrate. Concentrate. Con-

"Miss Wilson, don't even think about it," Shelly warns.

There's a young scream below me. Must be the girlfriend, which means he's right under me. I squeeze my eyes shut harder and open my hand to be ready to close around my creation.

"Dude, you're crazy!" the skater-boyfriend shouts.

Just watch how crazy it's about to get.

It appears.

I snap my eyes open. Before me he stands, balancing himself on the bar in front. Even though our cart has stopped moving, we are at the tip and I'm surprised he's not struggling to stay upright. His eyebrows are raised at the sword in my hand. Impressed. He might've been a little cute if he hadn't killed my sister and other innocent kids like Suzette and Davy. His arms and chest are big with strength. I remember the dent in his chin when he looked me in the eye four months ago and grabbed my sister out of my arms.

Don't admire him, Mariam.

I swipe the sword at his head. I suck, like real bad, and he easily ducks from it without falling off the bar or struggling to hold on.

"You wanna play?" he asks, his voice excited.

I don't answer, not even blink. Ike holds out his hand. A sword longer than mine flashes into his hand.

"Oh no," Shelly whispers. I had forgotten she was there.

Ike jumps down from the bar and into our cart. It tilts a lot and I have to hold on with my free hand like a loser. Shelly tries to get out of the way with Ike's back to her. He feels her behind him though, and gets greedy for his space. He shoves the agent roughly out of his way. Shelly loses her balance and slips, her body thrown backwards and right out of the cart. She lets out a small cry and, luckily, her hands catch onto the railing before it goes out of reach. Below, the bystanders watch, terrified for Shelly's life.

"Shelly!" I yell.

I try to reach for her, but Ike blocks my way. A cruel smile grows on his face. I look down. We're not even close to the ground.

The only way to get to Shelly is through Ike. Please God, help her hang on.

"Now, let's see who's better with a blade," Ike suggests, locking me in a corner.

He stabs his sword at me. He misses by an inch. He wouldn't miss, I thought. If he wanted me dead, I wouldn't be breathing right now. I swipe my sword at his neck. He catches my wrist with his free hand and squeezes it with hidden force and pulls it behind my back. I wince in pain. My sword drops from my hand and disappears while landing with a large light.

"I guess I'm the winner," he whispers in my ear.

I close my eyes and think of the first thing that comes to mind. Size: flat, hard, skinny. Color: brown. Smell: wood. Touch: rough, splinters.

Once it appears, I smash the wooden chair into Ike's head. He doesn't expect that and lets go of me, holding his face in his hands and cursing at the extra strength I gave the chair. He pushes himself against the other side of the cart. I hold the chair up and slam it back into his face once more. The chair breaks into a million pieces as Ike topples backwards and over Shelly's dangling body. The crowd screams and I shut my eyes from the blinding light as it snatches the chair away from existence. I grab Shelly's hands and pull her back up into the cart. After knowing she's safe and not hurt, I look over the edge of the cart for Ike's black hair. Amazed, my eyes are glued to him as he runs through the stream of people and into the parking lot. How the heck did her survive that fall?

After we get off the Ferris wheel, the ticket guy begs for our forgiveness. We quickly take it, knowing he was caught off guard. A couple of officers rush up to us and I stand to the side while Shelly speaks to them. After their conversation is over, half jogs towards the direction Ike left, and the other half jogs back the way they came. Once I and Shelly both leave the fairgrounds, I breathe out a sigh of relief.

"Thank you Jesus we lived through that," I say.

"Lived through it?" she repeats, looking way angry. "Far from."

"What are you talking about? I saved your life," I remind her.

"And destroyed yours. Miss Wilson, he was testing you. And you failed, terribly. He was not sure you had the power," she explains. "But now he is. And *now*, you're his next target."

CHAPTER 14

"Did he hurt you?" Ms. Bell asks me Sunday afternoon. We're in the library with her standing in front of me and her hands on the table, and me with my butt in a chair.

I shake my head and lean back farther in my seat.

"Did you hurt him?"

I shrugged. "He survived a fall that should've killed anyone."

"He has a very powerful mind. He could've made anything to protect his fall from a swimming pool to a trampoline."

"Shelly said that I'm his next target," I say. "She said he was only testing me at the fair."

"And she's probably right. We should get on with our last lesson."

I look at her. "Last?"

She nods. "And it's a very difficult one. I need all your concentration if you want to do this right and with no blood."

I watch as she pulls out two bottles of the blue liquid medicine. I shudder at the taste and Ms. Bell smiles at me as if she pulled out sweet candy instead.

"How hard exactly?" I ask, suspicious and a little scared. Just a little.

"You will learn how to form your creations at different spots," she said.

"You mean, *not* in the palm of my hand?"

"Correct."

I lick my lips before getting out of my seat. "Is this something Ike Henderson is able to do?"

Ms. Bell doesn't seem to need to think about the question. "Oh, I'm sure he knows a lot more than me."

I don't say anything. I hadn't wanted that to be the answer.

"Close your eyes," she directs. "Imagine a driveway. But not just any driveway. Your driveway. Every dirt or stain. If there's a certain bush in your front yard that helps you picture your driveway, than don't forget to put the bush in your picture. Throw in all the information you have."

I do the best I can. Sadly, there isn't a bush or tree or flower that helps me remember what my driveway looks like. Now that I'm thinking about it, it's starting to get real hard to see it in my head at all.

"Ms. Bell, I can't," I say, defeated. I keep my eyes closed.

"Then think of a memory," she suggests. "A very strong memory that you can see with your eyes shut tight."

A memory? I see the color green in the corner of my mind and I grab at the image. The color grows bigger and transforms into an object- into a dress. The dress flaps from a breeze and a small, fragile body appears, with the dress tight around its figure. I clench my fist. The body has a face and a smile comes forth with a tiny nose over it and dark brown eyes above that. I think about opening my eyes. But then I decide that this is exactly the memory I want.

The background forms and I can see the driveway perfectly. And with the smiling Erika in front of it, I realize she's the only information I need to remember.

"I've got it," I tell my tutor.

"Good. Hold out your hand towards the direction of the driveway. The better you get at designing things at different spots, the more you don't have to use your hand to point where it should go. Now create a car on your driveway," she commands.

My eyes still shut and hand out-stretched, I think up an easy car. Size: long, tall, round wheels, square windows. Color: tomato red, black, silver, see-through. Smell: metal, clean, new. Touch: smooth, squeaky clean, rough spiky wheels. Circled steering wheel, shinning headlights, leather car seats. Gas pedal, brakes, locks, a rearview mirror, and anything else that I don't know the name to.

Out of nowhere, I feel weight crashing over me. I choke on the pressure. But then it's gone in a second. I open my eyes.

"Did it work?" I ask.

Ms. Bell is already walking out of the room. "Let's find out."

I run to catch up and we both walk down the stairs and out the front door together. Once we step off the porch and turn a corner, we open up into the driveway.

A hot red truck stood in the driveway. Exactly the way I described it.

"Amazing," I mutter.

"Very good," Ms. Bell says, slowly circling the truck.

I stand beside her as she opens the hood. Inside is completely empty, looking like a large hole down into nowhere.

"But no engine," said Ms. Bell. She slams the hood shut and tries the driver's door handle. It doesn't open- locked. "Keys?"

"Sorry-" I start.

"It's okay. I didn't expect there to be an engine. Making stuff come to life, especially this huge, is complicated. More complicated for a young mind."

"I bet Ike could," I mumble so low that your ear had to be close enough to hear. I remember the car he had slam into me. Of course he can make things come to life, and even worse, form them at different positions like I'm learning to do right now. How did he get so great alone? Did he have someone teach him or is he just good at catching on to things?

I follow Ms. Bell back into the house, up the stairs, and into the library. We put everything back like it used to be: the rest of the tables in the middle, chairs circled around it, and the couches closer to the center of the room. Then I quietly watch her collect her things, thinking, that this is it.

I walk her to the front door. I give her a long hug, not letting go until she softly pushes me away. I tell myself not to cry. I tell myself really hard not to cry. To just keep it all in and let it burst when I'm locked in my room. It didn't go that way. Tears start to fall and my nose gets wet and my mouth begins to tremble. Ms. Bell is like my second mother. I hate the fact that someone who annoyed me so bad is such a good friend now, but I'm also glad I found another person I can trusts in my life.

Ms. Bell holds my face in her two, tender hands, forcing me to look straight into her eyes.

"Promise me," she says. "Just promise me one thing."

"Anything," I said.

"Stay alive. Please. Make sure you stay alive. I didn't teach you all that so you can die smart. I taught you that so you can live smart," she smiles.

"Ok. I promise," I say and return the smile. "But there's no reason I shouldn't be alive when you *do* visit."

Ms. Bell's smile slowly ebbs away. She would visit me, right? Maybe she really thinks Ike is on his way to kill me, no matter how far away he's murdering other kids.

I open the door and watch as she steps off the porch. I sniff up my tears. I have her number, I can call her whenever. Before she turns the corner, she twirls around, her face serious.

"Make sure you get some sleep. With more energy, your brain is more alive."

"I will," I say. Just not right now.

She turns the corner. I shut the door and lock it. I lean against the door. I feel for my cellphone in my back pocket. I sigh. If the answers no, I'll just keep calling until I hear a yes.

Scared, I take out my phone and punch in the seven digits. I press the phone to my ear. I hear the first ring. Second. Third. F-

"Hello?"

For a second, I don't speak, amazed that she picked up. "Hi. It's me."

"I know. What do you want?"

"Uhm. Are you free tonight?"

Moment of silence on the other end. "Maybe."

"I am," I tell her. "I want to hang out. Maybe go see a movie."

"Oh, now you want to hang out?" she asks, her voice on the brick of yelling at me.

"I'll explain everything. I promise."

She sighs, telling me she's frustrated. "Ok, whatever," Ashley agrees.

I stand in front of the theater, waiting for Ashley and May to show up. Outside, the weather is being irritating. There's a half moon and the wind hits me a little harder. Cold rain falls along with the wind. The worst combination of weather. I pull my hood up, which shields half of my vision. No one's outside except for me. I had already bought the tickets, so the workers are gone. It's just me out here in the rain and wind, the tips of my boots covered with snow.

Done deciding, I'm about to turn around and wait inside in the warmth, when a car's headlights flash in my face. I put up my hand to block some of the light and squint at the black car. It slowly drives past me. I try to look through the window to see who's driving the car. My heart skips a beat at the sight of Ike.

No, I'm just dreaming. It can't be him.

But when I see him grin behind the wheel, I know it is.

"Mariam?"

I jump at the sound of my name. I look right to see Ashley and May climb out of a white van and walk towards me. I look back where Ike is. His car is gone. You were hallucinating, I tell myself. But the smarter part of me knows better. My hand goes for my pocket to contact Shelly, but just then, May jumps in front of me. She pulls me into a hug and gives me a squeeze.

I squeeze her back.

Ashley's body stands frozen in front of me, holding a green umbrella in her hand. "Why are you standing outside in the rain?"

She doesn't wait for my answer. Ashley passes me up and walks inside the theater. May and I go in behind her, get our tickets ripped in half and told the direction to go to watch the movie we preferred. First, we get in line to buy some popcorn, smoothies, and sour candy. Chocolate for me, of course.

Ashley stays one step ahead of us.

"Don't worry," May assures me. "She's glad you called."

"Yeah, seems like it," I mutter real low.

Once we all enter the right room to watch the movie with our goodies, we find three empty seats in the middle and quickly snag them.

All throughout the waiting and the previews, we're quiet. When the movie starts and lights go dim, I turn my head to look at Ashley. My best friend in the world, I think in my head. She ignores my stare. I offer her some of my chocolate (something I never do). Inside, I smile bright when she takes a little and eats it. She offers her sour gummy worms to me. I take two.

Maybe it won't be as bad as I thought it would be.

"What kind do you want?" the lady with the high ponytail and wearing the stores shirt that says Cold & Good asks me, gesturing to all the different types of ice cream behind the see-through glass.

After the depressing movie was over, we drove to Cold & Good in Ashley's van. We didn't speak at all. May did, but it would be unnatural for her if she didn't.

"Uh, chocolate chip," I answer.

She takes her scooper and digs it into the chocolate chip ice cream and she lifts it out and drops the scoop into a colorful cup. I pay for it and sit across from May and Ashley in the booth. I grab a spoon out of the little container jailing them in. All three of us are speechless as me and Ashley swallow our ice cream off a spoon and May licks it from a cone.

I clear my throat. What I do to prepare for a lie to a friend.

"May, I think your makeup is fading."

She touches her cheek where her pink blush is. "Really?"

"Yeah, you should go check on it. In the bathroom," I add, trying to force it into her brain to go exactly there.

"Ok," she says, balancing her ice cream cone on the table. She slides out of the booth and hurries to the back of the ice cream shop, towards the bathroom.

Once she's out of hearing range, Ashley locks her eyes with mine. "She's not going to be in there long. And she can't hear this…how bad is it?"

"I'm working with the police," I blurt, quietly, even though the only worker is in the back room.

Ashley's eyes fly open wider. "Since when?"

"Since I screwed up May's birthday party."

"What for?"

Again, I'm whispering. "To finish family matters."

"You mean…to find your sister's murderers?" she asks.

I was tempted to tell her its murderer not murderers. But I don't. "Yes."

She shakes her head. "Mariam, I don't know. That's dangerous. Have you watched the news? What they did to that kid…" she stops talking, but she's rubbing her wrist, a faraway look in her eyes.

"I know. But I have to."

"But how about if they remember your face? Remember that you're the sister of the little girl they murdered?"

"I'm sure they won't." But while I said that, I'm thinking, how could he forget?

Ashley eats a bit of her peppermint ice cream. "I know why you're doing it. I would too. But…I don't want you getting hurt. They're extremely dangerous. I mean, do you know how many people they've killed?"

"Yeah, I know, they've been doing it for years. But this time they're going to be caught," I said.

The door opens, making us both jump. A woman and a little girl skip inside. The little girl smiles at me, as if we've been friends for the longest. Then all the ice cream catches her eyes and she forgets about me and runs up to the ice cream that's supposed to taste like cake mix. She runs her hands against the glass, drooling.

May comes out of the bathroom, her hair now in a perfect ponytail; make up better, looking refreshed. Disgusted at the dripping of her ice cream cone, she throws it away. There are no napkins so she goes back into the bathroom.

I finish my ice cream and look back at the child. The same lady scoops up the cake mix ice cream and drops it onto a sugar cone. The child's guardian buys the ice cream cone and goes to the door. Before walking outside, the woman turns to the little girl, probably her granddaughter. "Katie, go get some napkins. Don't want you making a big mess in the car."

The girl skips up to the metal tray where the napkins should be laying. But it's empty. She innocently looks to her left and to her right. She holds up her palm. In the blink of an eye, three, white napkins transport into her hand. My mouth drops open. She sees me looking and smiles. She sets one of the napkins on my table and disappears out the door.

My face freezes in place, eyes on the napkin. The view is broken when Ashley takes it off the table and wipes her chin where the last bit of ice cream was stuck.

"Ready to go?" she asks. I was almost about to ask if she had just witnessed what I did, but quickly vote against it. I'd either be branded crazy or there'd be a million of questions I do not want to answer.

So I close my mouth and nod quietly. We grab May from the bathroom and climb into Ashley's van. Except for the radio down low and May's talk about her makeup and everything else about her, the ride is sort of silent. I sit in the front and gaze out the window while Ashley drives and May gushes that a cute guy in her class is now calling her. When we get to her house, she's still talking about how smooth his hair is and how his eyes change color when he's under the sun and when he's not. She's even talking while she's climbing out of the car and walking up to her porch. But when she's gone and Ashley's driving me home, I'm wishing she was still with us, chatting about her dream boy.

Ashley stops the car in front of my house. I look around in the dark. Good- no black car in sight.

Before I could open the car door, Ashley's hand falls onto my wrist. Her brown eyes are so serious that I hold my breath.

"Please, just please…don't die. Don't leave me. Or May- it would kill her to lose someone like you. It would kill me too," she admits, weakly.

I give her a strong hug. "I'm not leaving anyone," I promise.

She breaks into the first smile tonight.

CHAPTER 15

Right after school, there's a huge surprise. Instead of my nonsocial driver that seems to have no life, it's my mom picking me up with Islamiat in the passenger seat. I hop inside the car happily and my mom gives me a smile through the rearview mirror. My mom insisted on taking us to the mall. Actually, she insisted after Islamiat quit begging. She starts the car and leaves the school, arriving at our destination in an easy seventeen minutes.

Once we entered the doors, I remembered the gold dress. Ever since the day Ms. Bell left the sticky notes, it's gotten easier and easier to remember things I've created. It's like being trained to remember each dream you have, and soon, you don't even have to force up the memory or write it down to be reminded of what you dreamt up last night.

I felt has if I should stay away from that store for some reason. But with every other one, I and my sister basically rooted. We'd jump in and out of each place, running our hands through clothes, over gold necklaces, and posing in front of mirrors with rich heels on our feet. Islamiat skips around like a bunny in the shoe store, picking up random shoes that aren't even her size from sandals to boots. She gets giddy when she spots shoes she *thinks* she likes. She walks out with five different pairs.

The last store we walk in is the best for me. It has shirts the perfect color with the perfect designs. Skinny jeans that glue to your thighs and legs were placed along the walls. Jewelry, beautiful gorgeous jewelry, filled up a corner of the store. Belts, scarves, and mini jackets covered up the left side of the wall, all different colors. The left wall is orange. The right wall is sky blue with the front and back wall a lime green. The ceiling, with its hanging fans scattered over it and silver light bulbs dangling, is a shiny, bubble bee yellow. The whole store made me feel like I was floating through a rainbow. There's even a leprechaun statue beside the entrance to the girl's dressing room.

I survey through the numerous dresses in blue and green. I take out a glowing, green dress and pull it off the hanger and hold it up in front of my face. It's pretty, not exactly my style with the sparkles glittering at the bottom. It certainly isn't ugly, but not for me. Something May would like.

Mom thought otherwise. "Why don't you try it on? You might actually like it with it on."

I shrug. "It couldn't hurt."

I take the dress with me into the dressing room. I grab the empty stall and lock myself in. Quickly, I change. Half naked, I lift the dress over my head and let the soft fabric flow over my shoulders and down around my waist. It stops after my ankles. Long, sparkly, and it made me feel like I was about to get married. Which I surely do not want to think of right now. I rip the dress off my body and hurriedly pull my jeans and shirt back on. I fix my hair and pull open the door. The lights in the store magically shut off.

Before I could take one step, a dusty sack falls over my head. The scent from the sack runs into my lungs, and I began to choke. Strong, sharp hands grab my wrists and hold them behind my back. I try to scream, but the more I open my mouth, the easier it is for the scent to cruise inside my body. I know it's some type of drug trying to make me sleepy; pass out. Or just kill me.

Either way, I couldn't feel my legs, I couldn't feel my arms. I wasn't sure anymore if my eyes were opened or closed. My heart beats twice as fast. My throat burns. I trip off my feet.

Paralyzed.

Death.

Is it supposed to hurt like hell? Cause it sure does. Or am I not dead? Maybe I'm dreaming. Yeah, dreaming. I remember falling asleep in sixth period and maybe I haven't woken up yet. Maybe I dreamt going to the mall with Islamiat and Mom.

But can you smell in dreams? Can you even feel pain in dreams? Wait, maybe I'm not dreaming. Maybe I really am dead. Maybe, maybe, maybe. I should be used to that word. I was never told the answers I wanted to know.

I blink. At least, I think I did. I can feel my eyelash flap against my skin under my eye. But still, I can't see the white walls in my room or the brown fan hanging from the ceiling. Or my dusty alarm clock, which I never touched, never used, because I'm so used to waking up at six.

But you breathe when you're alive. Your heart beats. Your lips twitch. Your skin shivers when you're cold.

Cold. I can feel wind. Not much, to where you knew you were outside, but enough to know there's a window open to your…to my left. I try to wiggle my fingers. They actually move. I stretch my palm out. My left thumb feels a thick string around my wrists. I'm bounded.

I start to squirm. I do my best to rip apart my two wrists from each other. It's not working. And it almost feels like the binds are pushing into my skin even tighter.

I feel a cold hand touch my elbow. Oh my God, I think. I freak out. I scream. At least, I try to, but tape is spread across my lips. I try to pick up my feet. Tied. No! No! I want to scream. This can't be happening.

A sack is yanked off my face. Hesitantly, I let my eyes open.

My legs are stretched out in front of me. Ankles together, tied with a large rope. I'm in a house. No, a building. Empty building except for me and a lamp on the other side of the room. It gives a little light. One window, off to my left, the one that's open.

A large figure leans over me. I feel like a five-year old for a moment, thinking it's the boogeyman standing before me. Then I remind myself I'm seventeen and I should at least act my age before I die. Long, black hair blocks his eyes, though I know he can see me. A smile grows on his face. A smile I recognized when I was on a date with Dillon. A smile I recognized at the fair. A smile I recognized at the theater. A smile I recognized when he stole my sister.

I try to scream. I try to scream as loud as I can. But it comes out as a moan because of the tape stuck to my face. I struggle with the rope on my wrists.

"The more you struggle, the tighter it gets."

His voice. Oh God, the voice that gave me nightmares to scare an adult. A voice that almost made my heart jump out of my mouth when he said, "I'm just like her".

I stop battling with the rope because I believed him. The rope has started to pierce into my skin. I feel liquid drip between my fingers. Surely my blood.

Calm down, Mariam. Calm down, I whisper in my head. I breathe slowly through my nose. I suck in my tears. My hearts still beating faster than a dog's chase after a cat. But at least my fear and pain isn't showing. It also proves I'm not dead. Aren't I lucky?

Ike stares into my face. Don't blink, I think. He doesn't either. After two minutes of neither of us moving, glaring into each other's eyes, he breaks into an impressed grin.

"You're good. I like you. You're almost like me," he says.

I don't laugh, though I'm sure he wanted me to.

He's still talking, as if were long-lost buddies having a chat over coffee. "We're both tricky; no one knows what we're going to do next. We don't look so bad either. We both just want to survive in this world. And our brains clearly have the same strength." He leans in closer. "It's kind of difficult to kill your twin." He rests on the floor beside me, our shoulders touching which makes me flinch and my binds around my wrists grow tighter. "But," he begins again, "with one of them tied up and strapped, well, then there's no competition."

Now he's grinning like he's about to get lucky. Except I know he's thinking much worse.

He holds out his palm. A long, sharp blade, longer than my arm, appears in his hand. He holds the rectangular handle with his one hand and feels around my leg. I try my best not to shiver, but I lose. He doesn't get perverted (thank God), and just explores my knee and below. I want to scream when I see him hold up the blade like he's about to slice me with it.

"Did you watch the news?"

I don't move and still can't speak.

"Davy Newton. Easiest I've ever killed," he says, shaking his head at his good work. "The kid was a retard. He basically told me where he lived."

I'm disgusted.

Ike's face then scrunches up as if he smelt something foul. He moves his hand away from my leg and holds up his weapon. He brings it to my face, placing the blade against my cheek. I hold my breath.

"You know what makes me mad?" he asks. The point of the blade digs into my skin a little just below my eye. "I've been at this for more than two years and you guys still call me by my real name." He slides the blade down towards my lips, the cold metal like an icicle burning your skin before it breaks loose and sticks itself into you.

"I'm not expecting a name like Jack the Ripper or The Sunday Morning Slasher. I guess I'm not important enough because I don't keep my victims heads in my closet or do rituals where I dance around in my underwear while they burn over a fire. I just kill and leave. How boring. But I deserve a name, don't I? *Don't I?*"

If that makes you happy, I thought of saying if my mouth wasn't taped shut.

The blade cruises down my neck and to my shoulder blades. I squirm under my binds, leaning away from the weapon. Ike keeps speaking, looking as if his arm has a mind of its own.

"So I've decided to give myself a name. Nothing too big, but fetching enough. I thought of how much I don't care who you are and that you can't run away from me. And then I realized," he laughs loud and harsh like a maniac, "the perfect name was right there!"

I struggle to twist away from the blade while it travels past my breasts, down to my waist, and over to my left leg. Holding my breath wasn't a very good idea, because now I'm panting, freaking scared I'm going to die.

"The Callous Catcher," he said, his eyes bright and awake. "It sounds good, doesn't it? It sounds just right."

He suddenly clutches my leg with his large hand, an inch under my knee. He rolls up my pants at the ankles until it gives him the room he needs. Needs for him to cut off my foot!

He holds up the blade over the spot he chose. "I'm goanna make you bleed out. And I'm going to watch with a smile on my face."

Now's the time to scat.

I shut my eyes.

Size: long, sharp, skinny. Color: silver. Touch: sharp, flat part smooth. Scent: metal.

I picture the spot in front of Ike with the dangerous blade about to chop off my precious foot. I picture my weapon stabbing Ike in the forehead.

I feel something prick my right palm and soar past my ear. Ike cries out in pain and a bright light snatches the murderer's weapon away. My binds and tape break off and vanish. I open my eyes.

Ike's holding his forehead, yelling and cursing. I try to stand up, but he grabs my wrist. I scream. Blood's pouring down his face in a line from a long cut in the middle of his forehead. Dang it, I've only given him a scratch.

But that was enough to make him angry.

He pushes me against the wall, banging my head into it. I kick his kneecap. He doesn't even wince. He brings his hands around my throat. He squeezes. I throw a knife. It scratches him in the neck. He releases one of his hands to cover his scratch. I take that time to do my part.

Again, I kick him in the kneecap. But I don't stop at that. I punch my elbow in his throat. He gags for a short minute. I grab at his fingers, doing my best to pull them off my throat. I'm starting to get dizzy.

The murderer's breath is hot and smells like Chinese food as he breathes in my face.

"Did they really think someone like you could kill me?" he wonders.

I gasp for air. My arms flail wildly, and my eyes are so wide with terror that I'm afraid they'll pop out.

"You're so small and young," he says. "I can't believe how desperate they are."

A black shadow begins to grow wider, blocking my vision. This time, it looks like the real boogeyman and that he's about to eat me.

"Please," I choke.

He heard the word and smiles a little.

Finally, I can breathe again. Ike's hand is gone and the boogeyman decided to save me for dessert.

I drop to my knees and massage my bruised throat. My throat is dry and my neck is burning. I was about to die. I was about to die and I told my sister's murderer please. The question is, was I telling him please to hurry and finish me off, or to let me live. Because with him standing in front of me right now, wanting to be alive sounds like a terrible idea.

"What I keep wondering is, do you hate me so much that you'd let them waste your life on trying to kill me?"

I look up at him, holding my neck in my hands. I sound like I'm losing my voice when I speak.

"I don't know what you mean."

Ike is very tall with me on my knees and him on his feet. He steps forward.

"Did she mean that much to you?" he asks.

I swallow. "She was my sister. She meant a lot."

He nods slowly. "So now you're doing as much as you can to kill me. Even going along with the dumbest idea I've ever heard."

"I don't-" I loudly cough- "I don't understand."

"Don't lie to my face." He comes nearer.

"I'm not. I'm not lying."

He stops and squints. And then grins.

"Oh," he says. "So that's how they play."

"Who?"

"Your dear friends. Especially that one agent. God, she gets on my nerves."

"Playing what? I'm confused," I admit.

"Yeah I would be too while trying to fix the lies with the truth," he said.

"There…there are no lies."

"You're so dumb to think they're trying to protect you."

"They are," I defend.

"Please," he says, waving his hand through the air as if to swat a fly. "Think about it, girl. Every day they're trying to perfect you. *Why*?"

"So I'll learn how to master my gift," I quickly shut my mouth only because that's the first time I ever called it "my gift".

"You don't *need* them. Or that dumb therapist. I taught myself my gift all by myself. And look how I turned out."

I sit up straighter. "Yeah, look at you. You live alone in an abandon building and you kill young kids. You murder people."

"And what the hell do you think their trying to teach you right now?"

My mouth shakes as I struggle to find the right words to say.

"That annoying agent is the smartest out of all of you," he shakes his head at my foolishness. "Even smart enough to trick you. She's darn right about her theory. I am moving to the next city. Only, I realized today that I missed one little duck. I don't know how she hid from my radar, but she's not hiding anymore."

I couldn't move. I didn't know what to say. I could hardly think straight. Lies. Murder. One last duck. I didn't know what to believe, take as a distraction, and what to fight for. Shelly, Ike, and one last duck.

"I decided that while I'm still here, I might as well take care of you too. Get you out of the way before they send you out," he said.

"Send me where?" I ask.

"To kill me of course."

My jaw drops.

"Damn, you really don't know, do you?"

"Then why don't you tell me," I suggest with my body stiff.

He licks his lips. "They're only using you. Why do you think they were so excited to find you? Why do you think that agent wanted you so bad?"

"Her name is Shelly," I correct.

"Oh, I know her name." He smiles once again. "I know all their names. The agent. The therapist and scientist. Even the FBI dude. You don't know how much I keep an eye on the people that get in my way."

"We're only trying to stop you," I said.

"Which makes you in my way. I know how mad you are that I killed your sister. But I'm going to do you a favor. You can be with her."

A cruel looking dagger appears in his hand. The blade is sharp and deadly. Ike picks up his feet, coming right to me.

This time, I don't shut my eyes, I just think hard, giving my power all I've got.

Size: no shape, no size. Color: orange, red. Smell: burnt. Touch: hot, burns, stings.

I aim it at Ike's chest.

I feel a quick tingle of heat spread inside my palms. A ball of fire smacks into Ike's chest, sizzling all around. His dagger immediately disappears. He falls on the ground and screams. I'm not sure what he did next, because I'm already gone, looking for an exit.

I realize it's an empty underground warehouse than an empty building. I run into a hallway and find stairs leading up. I climb them and shove open a large door. Fresh air almost knocks me down. Happy, I run out into the open air.

My mind's still connected to the fire (maybe he's burnt to a crisp now). I do my best to keep it alive, but something else is trying to destroy it. Could be water. Either way, it's making my head hurt a lot. I stop running and think of burnt marks on Ike's body. I think it over and over again, while trying to keep my head straight at the same time. I feel a short pain in my gut, but it's gone in two quick seconds. I sigh with relief that blood didn't show this time and I let the fire go, hopefully leaving a life-lasting mark.

I start walking hastily away from the warehouse. I wrap my arms around myself and jump onto the sidewalk. Where the heck am I?

To my left is emptiness. To my right are the woods, which look darker somehow when it doesn't even have much trees. It looks like it keeps going on and on. I stare up at the moon. It's big and bright. There are no stars, but a plane is flying.

I feel my back pocket. My phones gone. Great, now the murderer can text all my friends. Maybe he'll call Dillon and give him boyfriend advice. "You know how to make them fall in love with you?" he'd say. "You grab them by the throat and squeeze. Girls *love* that kind of stuff."

I shiver.

Up ahead, I'm sure I can see lights. Town, neighborhood, store? Just as long as there's people.

It ends up being a vacant gas station. Two street lights are on beside it, giving me enough light to lead myself to the phone booth. I had no quarters in my pocket, but no worries, I just make one. I pick up the phone, wipe the mouth piece and ear piece with my sleeve, punch in the number of the only person I know would be awake at one in the morning, and press the phone to my ear.

It rings twice before I hear a relaxed voice answer.

"Hello?"

"Charmaine, its Mariam. Can you come get me?" I ask, a bit of begging in my voice.

"Right now?" she asks, clearly surprised.

"Yes. Please."

"Of course," she says.

I tell her where I am the best I can. She promises to be here as soon as possible.

It takes her an hour. Not because she had complications finding me. It's because I'm actually an hour away from home.

When I get into her boyfriend's car, she realizes how jacked I look and tells me to take a nap. She asks me what I was doing around her. I wouldn't tell her, so she guessed a party. Actually, I did look like I came from a crazy party.

I go to sleep.

When I wake up, the sun isn't up yet but I'm glad to see us driving through my neighborhood. I lean my head against the window. My body feels dead. My mind's cloudy. It's a little harder to think straight. I wasn't aware of how much it took out of me to create that fire. *Making stuff come to life is complicated. More complicated for a young mind.*

Charmaine pulls into my driveway and turns to me with the car still running.

"Mariam, you know you can use this car whenever you feel like it," she tells me.

"Your boyfriend wouldn't mind?" I ask, not entirely sure I even want to use his car.

She shakes her head. "No, he's cool with it. You know, as long as you bring it back in one piece."

"Right. Thanks for picking me up."

She shrugs. "It's not like I was busy you little party animal." I'm about to give her a thank-you hug when I watch her face drop.

"What happened to your neck?"

My hand immediately goes to my throat. I hold back a wince once I touch my skin. "What do you mean?"

"Well, that doesn't look like any hickey I've even seen. It looks like someone strangled you."

She picks up her hand to feel the bruises but I lean back without even meaning to. She drops her hand.

"Are you okay?" she asks. Charmaine's never worried. Why did she look so worried now?

"I'm fine," I retort. "Thanks again."

I jump out of her car before she's able to stop me. I unlock the door to my house and walk inside. The whole three-story building is dark and quiet except for the kitchen. I shut the front door softly and make my way there.

Pacing back and forth is my mom. She is in her robe, her hair tied back in a messy bun. She looks like she's been crying. Oh no, what have I done?

"Mom," my voice is barely a whisper, "I'm sorry…"

"Mariam!" she shouts loud enough to wake the whole house.

"Where have you been?"

"I'm sorry," I repeat. "I s-saw my friends in the mall. I mean, didn't you get my message?"

"What message?"

"The one I sent to your phone," I lie. My hands are in fists because this is something I hate doing.

"No, I didn't get any messages. You wouldn't even answer your phone when I called." She shakes her head as if to throw away the conversation we're having. "Don't ever do that again. You scared me half to death."

"I'm sorry-"

"It felt like it was happening all over again," she whispers. "When the lights turned back on in the store and you weren't there."

I stare at her. "I won't do it again. I promise. I'm sorry," I repeat.

She pretends she doesn't hear me. She looks at my outfit, her face tight and disgusted. "Go upstairs and put those clothes in the hamper. Then go to sleep. You look like you came from a party and rolled in dirt."

Walking up the stairs to my room, I silently apologize to Mom for lying to her. I hate lying to her. I promised never to. It sucks when you break a promise you made to yourself.

But I couldn't tell her the truth. Because if I did, it might just ruin her.

CHAPTER 16

The next day, I skip school. I wake up on time and dress. I jump in the car and tell the driver where I want to go. He listens, but I think it's because he knows I'm mad and ready to blow someone's head off. I even told him to step on the gas just a little harder before I yell and sprint to the building myself.

Once we're here, I march pass the short lady at the desk. She never really made eye contact with me. But this time, she looks the minute she realized I'm not about to sign in to make an *appointment* with Shelly. She hops out of her seat and blocks my path.

"Do you have an appointment?" she questions.

"No," I answer. I move to the right. The midget moves with me.

"You need to make an appointment to see her."

I put my hands up. "Lady, you really don't want to mess with me right now. I will step on you if you don't get out of my way."

She swallows. I walk around her but she follows in pursuit.

"She's having a meeting right now," she tries. "You can't just walk in."

Watch me.

I swing the door open.

Ms. Bell's back is to me but she turns around then. Shelly gets up from behind her desk, folding her hands together.

"Miss Wilson," she says.

"I'm sorry. I tried to stop her-"

"You can go, Amy."

Amy nods and shuts the door behind her.

"Miss Wilson, how can I help you?" the agent asks.

"You can start by telling me the truth," I say, stepping forward. I try not to look at Ms. Bell. With her present, it's harder to do what I planned. But, I am a lot angrier than I've ever been.

"What do you mean?"

"The truth, Shelly. Don't you know what that is? Tell me why you're really helping me."

"I don't know if you've forgotten, Miss Wilson, but you had almost killed yourself a while ago," said Shelly.

"Sooner or later, I would realize what's happening and teach myself how to control it," I say, remembering Ike. He taught himself and he's even better than I am.

"This way, with Ms. Bell as your tutor, is safer."

"Yes, because that's exactly what you care about. My safety. Smells like crap and you know it."

Shelly drops her head. She places her fingers on her desk as if to steady herself.

"I see you know. I was going to tell you."

"When?" I demand. "When he's standing in front of me with a gun? When I'm *dead*?"

"The day I brought everyone to the lab. But Malcolm was there."

"No, don't blame this on Malcolm. You should've told me the moment I got into your car the first time," I point my finger at her. "I trusted you, Shelly. And here you are, planning on setting me in front of the murderer. He will *kill* me."

"That's why we train," Shelly picks up her voice. "That's why we're teaching you to know how to use your gift."

"I can't believe you," I mutter. "I'm sixteen. I haven't even lived my life yet. I've tried to do everything you asked of me."

Because I want to make you happy. But I'm not going to tell her that.

Shelly sighs like a winner recognizing themselves losing. "I thought you'd be honored to be given this part."

Considering I have a grudge on Ike Henderson. Or that it's my fault my sister's gone, gone forever. Maybe she thinks I'm so mad that I'll do whatever it takes, even risking my life, to delete him from this world. That I'll kill him with my bare hands if I have to.

"You thought wrong," I respond.

She looks away, working her jaw.

I said what I had to say, so I turn around to leave. Only, Ms. Bell's in my way. She puts her hands on my shoulders.

"I'm so proud of you," she tells me. There are tears in her eyes. "You do what you want. But don't forget to fight for what you believe in."

I slip out of her arms and get to the door. I hold the cold handle in my hand, squeezing it.

"I know his next target," I said.

I hear Shelly suck in her breath. "How?" she wonders.

Tell her, I thought. Tell her everything right now. Explain how you got kidnapped and admit you know his hideout.

I shut my eyes. "I just do. Her name is Katie. She's eight or seven. I suggest you keep a tight lock on her. He's not leaving until she's taken care of."

Shelly nods. "You did well."

"I didn't do it for you," I tell her.

When I leave, I feel like crying.

Trusting people is a mistake.

On Wednesday, I went to school like I should. I also put on a turtle neck to screen the bruises. I saw them in my mirror, purple and black, almost exactly the same shape as Ike's fingers. It still hurt when I touched it and it didn't feel so great when I turned my head too fast.

At lunch, Dillon sat with us. It was awkward at first because it was always us three. And no boys. We didn't know what to talk about with him around, especially sitting right next to me. Dillon *was* one of the things we talked about.

Ashley breaks the ice. She brings up her stepdad and how he's planning on training boys to box. With his injured leg, he has to stop the professional boxer he is. Once Dillon learned his name, his eyes lit up. He then starts going on about watching Ashley's stepdad when he was younger. He was his favorite. Dillon looks like a cute puppy when he's excited.

But lunch was easy to help me forget. Forget the lies and the betrayals. I'm not even mad Ike kidnapped me anymore. If he hadn't, I'd still be following along Shelly's plan like paparazzi stalking a star.

And the fact that Ms. Bell knew. Whose side is she on?

I was never sure if Shelly did anything about Katie. I know I made it sound like I didn't ever want to speak to the agent again, but I'd like to know if the little girl was alright. There's nothing on the news about a dead kid, but the police does everything possible to make sure the world is unaware about Ike Henderson.

I find out everything I wanted to the next day.

Islamiat barges into my room. "You have a visitor."

I look up from doing my homework on my bed.

"Who?"

"Some lady," she shrugs.

Ms. Bell? Shelly? Ms. Bell? Shelly?

It's Shelly. I watch her a few seconds as she waits for me in the entryway alone. I walk down the stairs, and when I'm in front of her, I'm still holding my breath.

It's full of snow outside and it's all over her jacket and boots. But her hair is dry and make up tip-top. She seems to transform into an artist when you hand her eye linear and eye shadow.

Then I notice the lumps under her eyes. The way she's leaning on her right leg as if she doesn't trust her left leg to hold her up. And her gun around her waist, deliberately showing it to the world.

Something went horridly wrong.

"I don't know how you knew, Miss Wilson," talks Shelly. "But you were right."

"Katie," I swallow.

Shelly looks away.

"Tell me," I order.

"She's hurt badly, but fine. That little girl is going to live because of you."

She puts weight on her left leg and struggles to hide her obvious wince.

I lick my lips. "And what happened to you?"

She looks down at her injured leg. "Nothing. A piece of glass got stuck in my leg."

"How?"

"Ike Henderson. He had a bomb on him and I was standing in front of a window when he let it blow. He hurt my men also. We all guarded Katie at her grandmother's house. He knew we were there. He knew we were there the whole time."

"How would he know?"

"I don't know. But Miss Wilson-"

"Doesn't make any sense," I mutter.

"Miss Wilson."

I shut my mouth.

"Katie's grandmother. She's dead."

"D-dead?"

"Ike. He…he shot her," she reveals.

I stare at her to make sure she's telling the truth. She looks dead serious.

"I want to see her," I said.

"I'll take you," Shelly offers.

"No, I want to go alone."

Her shoulders drop a little. "Okay. It's the hospital by the river."

"Alright," I said.

I watch Shelly leave my house.

I want to go alone. Solid excuse. Not the truth, but good enough. I rather not have Shelly around me, following behind or planning my day.

I think of Katie alone in a hospital room, maybe with a leg broken or a cut needing stitches. Does she know that her grandmother is gone? Did she catch Ike's face like I did and did he tell her something that will haunt her dreams forever?
Like me will she always be afraid to trust and do what she believes in?

I take Jamui's car for the second time. I speed to the hospital. Nothing looks different or out of the ordinary. There aren't twenty cop cars or anxious reporters. The parking lot is just as boring as a sleeping cat.

Which also means no one knows a little girl almost died today.

Inside the hospital, I don't go to the front desk. I had a feeling the receptionist won't tell me what room she's in. The cops would've warned her to keep it a secret unless a badge is shown. If she's smart enough, she'd listen.

So I pass up the desk like I know where I'm going and walk straight to the elevator. She's not on the first floor. I would've seen at least one cop if she was. And I believe the higher, the better.

I ride the elevator to the top floor.

On the highest level, I go left, checking the people I past and the noise coming from behind the closed doors. Slowly, memories flood back into my head and I'm tugging on the sleeve of my jacket, stretching it and agitating the taut seams.

I remember the good things first. The food wasn't too bad. The nurses were pretty sweet to me and my doctor made sure I was well. On the outside at least. Because I kept *every*thing inside. The dreams. The fears. Ike Henderson.

It had felt like the more I was in the hospital, the dreams- the nightmares- got worse. And after I met Shelly, I would literally wake up screaming. One time a nightmare was so bad that I believed a nurse trying to calm me down was Ike waking me up to kill me. I punched her in the head and she was referred to her own room in the hospital. I thought of buying her a card in the gift shop but I didn't know what to write on it except, "My bad for socking you. I was pretty sure you were about to murder me."

After that accident, they allowed me to go home and handed my parents a card with Ms. Bell's number on it.

Katie's room is at the end of the hall.

The tension gives it away. There are only two officers out of the ten men. The other eight are in suits, but guns at their waists all the same. Their backs aren't against the wall; they're more in three groups, discussing in whispers. They don't notice me as I listen intently and get closer and closer to Katie's door.

"He came up from behind me."

"He didn't have a gun. And then he did."

"We weren't prepared. We weren't prepared at all."

"Something's not right about this one."

"Who are you?" a voice demands.

I stop as a cop steps in my way before I get too close to the door. His eyes are mean and his mustache looks painted over his lips. He crosses his arms, which helps make him look taller and a little more frightening.

"Uh," I say to his questions.

"She's with me."

Malcolm appears beside me. I'm glad to see him, but only because I have no good reason of why I'm here. And when the cop sees who's talking, he walks away and enters a random group conversation.

I face Malcolm. He looks unscathed, a lot better than Shelly. Though he looks tired and his suit is wrinkled, I know he wasn't at Katie's house with the other cops.

"I think I have you to thank," he said.

I smile a little. "I just wanted to see her. And then I'll leave, I promise."

"Relax. We're not busy."

"But he might come back," I say without thinking.

Malcolm's the only one that heard me.

"How did you know?"

I look away.

He touches my arm. A friendly gesture but I still shiver.

"Mariam, you can tell me."

Yes, tell him. Tell someone!

I sniff. "I don't know who to trust."

"Whatever you say will never be repeated from my lips. That's a promise," he said.

Say it. Speak at least half of it.

But I turn away more, something that I should not have done. His fingers go to the bruises on my neck and I jump once our skin touches.

"Who did this to you?" he questions.

"Nothing. No one. I'm fine," I force the words out. I raise the collar on my jacket and step farther back. Malcolm's mouth is in a thin line, considering asking questions or allowing me to keep my secret. I open my mouth before he decides to hit me with arduous questions.

"Why weren't you there with Shelly?" I say.

"She told me to stay out of her way, remember. So that's what I did. But I should've been there. My men and I should've been there," he nods as if realizing how good of an idea it is.

"You and your men are here now," I point out.

"That's because Shelly doesn't want to risk the rest of hers."

"How come?"

Malcolm bites his upper lip. "Shelly had twenty-two men on that house. Five are dead, two lost a leg, and one's in a coma."

"Oh my God," I lean against the wall.

"The rest are fine, I suppose. But Shelly doesn't want to put them in jeopardy again."

"So what, she thinks she's just going to help herself?"

"I guess so."

She's crazy, I thought. Ike will kill her the moment she steps into the light.

"Has she said anything?" I ask, indicating to the child in the room.

"No. She doesn't want to talk," he answers.

"Does she know?"

"I would think so. I was told her grandmother was shot in front of her face."

Poor girl. That image will never leave her head.

"Let me talk to her," I said.

"Be my guest," Malcolm opens the door for me and I walk right in.

At least the room doesn't smell like dying people. It's a small square space with an opened window, two chairs and a bathroom. There's a vase with flowers and a lamp. Double nightstands on either side of the bed and a hanging T.V. across from that. In the bed is a little girl that likes cake mix ice cream and skipping along with her dead grandma.

The covers are to her chin, but you can see the injuries. The top of her head is wrapped. Her cheek is bruised, a big, purple bump, and her arm has a huge Band-Aid on the side. You're able to see blood underneath it as clearly as if the Band-Aid isn't even there.

She's also awake and giving me a look that means nothing at all.

I take a chair and carry it to the bed. I don't get too close to her. Maybe she'll notice the personal space I'm giving her and be easy on me. I slowly breathe out.

"Do you remember me?" I ask.

She stares.

"My name is Mariam Wilson."

Nothing. I never noticed how dark and dull her eyes are until now.

"I just want to talk. I'm not here to force you to be happy or gain information Katie."

Her hand twitches this time but I'm still going a useless direction. Changing my tactic would be a good idea.

I stand up and open my hand. Size: as wide and large as my chest. Arms and legs and ears and a nose. Color: brown fur, black eyes, red bowtie. Touch: soft, furry, and warm.

A brown stuffed bear appears in my clutches in a wink. Immediately, Katie's eyes become sprightly and she sits up in her bed.

"What part are you surprised by, Katie?" I question, gently. "That someone else is like you? That a random girl you saw in an ice cream shop can do what you can?"

She doesn't say anything. I drop the bear on her lap and she picks it up. I ignore my chair and sit on the edge of the bed.

"There's nothing to be afraid about," I tell her. Her hair looks damp close up and her fingernails have been bitten till bleeding.

"If you're afraid he'll come back, I'll stay with you. I wouldn't let him hurt you."

She pats the bears head. It doesn't even seem like she's listening to me.

"Just because your grandma's gone doesn't make you alone. He'll have to go through all of us to try to kill you again."

"He wasn't trying to kill me."

I'm sure I heard wrong. "What?"

"He didn't want to hurt me," she lifts the bear's arm and strokes the bowtie.

"That doesn't make any sense. Why would he come to you?"

"He wanted my help," she answers naturally.

"But your just...your just a little girl."

"That's exactly what he said."

I lose the lock and the bear disappears. Katie leans back with her hands empty.

"I'm sorry," I apologize, rubbing my forehead while the other one clinches into a fist.

"Why are you angry?" asks Katie.

"Why am I angry? Five men have died trying to protect you and you weren't even in danger."

"I didn't ask for them to protect me," she sinks into her mattress.

"I know. *I* did because I didn't want anything to happen to you."

"But you don't even know me," she points out.

'*You don't even know me'*. That's right, I don't know her, but I figured she was my responsibility because I was the one who knew her future. And I was wrong about that.

"What, exactly, did he want you to help him with?" I probe.

"He said he likes my age," she says. "He said I look very innocent. He said they would never expect it to be me."

"To do what?"

She meets my eyes. "To kill you."

I jump up from the bed and move towards the window. Katie sits up higher and reaches out her hand to me.

"Please don't," she begs. "I don't want to do it. I told him no. And then he said I'm better off dead and tried to kill me."

She begins to cry; crystal tears and shaking shoulders. Her nose goes wet and her hair gets in her face.

She could be pretending. For all I know, she could already be Ike's little pet, his young killer. He could be controlling her and she'd listen to every word. I can almost see the puppet-strings right now.

Only, she's about seven with a wounded heart and a bruised face. I go back to her side and put my arms around her. It feels just like it had felt with Saultan. The tears damping my shirt and the quavering shoulders that make my body tremble along with it.

"He killed my grandma," she whines.

I hold her tighter.

"She's all I had."

"I know," I kiss the top of her head.

Her arms are wrapped around my waist and her face on my shoulder. "Why does he want to kill me? I haven't done anything to him."

"He's just mad that you can do what he can. That we can do what he can," I said.

She lets me go and looks at me with red eyes and baby cheeks. "Take it out of me."

"That's not possible."

"Take it out the same way you got it in you."

"How do you know about that-"

"Please. I don't want to die," she gives me those pleading eyes and I feel myself give consideration to the thought. Then I remember what's right and what's wrong and realize that that's a very stupid and risky idea. And it won't work.

"I'm not going to let you do that. What's in your head is a part of you. That's what makes you who you are. Stop treating it like a curse or a sign of death. Treat it like it is. A gift Katie."

She bows her head.

I create a flower. No stem or leaves. Just pink petals and white in the middle. I drop it in her hand.

"It will always be nothing but a gift," I said.

Another one appears, not from my head. I look at Katie and she smiles up at me.

I lightly shut the door behind me and breathe out from my nose. Malcolm stashes his phone in his pocket. He leaves the wall he's trying to hold up and comes to my side.

"You look tired," he comments.

"So do you," I comment back.

He tugs up his jeans and crosses his arms. "What did she say to you?"

I shake my head like I still can't believe it. "She wasn't in any real danger. At least at first."

"Then why would he risk his life to go to her?"

"I think his goal was to kill her. But then he saw it as an opportunity to kill me."

"He asked a little girl to kill you?" ask Malcolm, eyebrows scrunched.

"Yes. But he didn't think she'd say no," I said. "He thought he'd scare her into murdering someone."

"Damn," the FBI agent mutters. He rubs his eyes with his large hand. "This guy must be bored. Now he's trying to recruit young assassins."

Or he must be really, really angry that I escaped. I get Goosebumps and cross my arms to hide them.

"I've tried contacting Shelly," he said. "She's not answering."

"No offense," I say, "but you're not really her favorite person."

It's hardly called a smile but the corner of his lips turn up.

"She seems to really like you. Trust you."

Don't get me started about trust, I think to myself.

"Will you do me a favor and call her."

"Um," I go.

"I'm really worried about her. I shouldn't be, because our relationship is over and we shouldn't care, but…"

He doesn't finish. I awkwardly pat his arm.

"Just because you guys broke up doesn't mean you shouldn't care about one another," I said. "I'll call."

This time, it's more of a smile. "Thanks."

"One more thing," I said. There's always something on my chest that I need to get off or I won't be able to sleep at night. "Ike Henderson knows who you are."

He blinks at me. I can see him wanting to ask how I'd possibly know that but he's biting his tongue.

"Shelly and Ms. Bell and Dr. Jeff also," I add.

He licks his lips. "What do you think I should do?"

"Warn them. And please keep them safe. You too."

"What about the girl?"

"She shouldn't be alone at any moment. Ike knows he didn't finish the job and that makes him angry."

"And you?"

I stare at him. "Me what?"

"Don't act like that. I know you're in as much danger as the rest of us. You are the one he tried to get a little kid to assassinate. I'm going to send a guard to your house," he decides.

I tense up. "No!"

He's surprised by my outburst.

"My family has no idea what I'm doing right now," I explain.

"They should know. You're putting them at risk," he says.

"I know. But Ike's not going to hurt them," I said.

"How do you know?"

"Because he already did his damage when he murdered my sister on the street."

Malcolm watches me for a moment. I try to look as calm and natural as possible.

"There will just be one," he said. "He won't show himself."

I groan.

"Your family won't notice him, I promise. This is to keep them safe, Mariam. I'm tired of going to funerals."

I catch the sorrow in his eyes. He's done losing people. He's ready to help some live. I nod at his idea to show my agreement. He holds out his hand.

I shake it.

CHAPTER 17

I did as I said I would. I call Shelly. I call her once I get home from the hospital. I thought not to, but decided it's smarter to try. I would hate myself if I never call her and find her gone forever.

Even though I tried, she didn't pick up. Three calls only led me to leaving three voicemails. Then I threw the phone at the wall because I hate being rejected. She didn't call back at all that night.

The last day of school for winter break was a long one. I'm sure it was because I was so terribly bored. The four periods before lunch were horrible. Two tests, a boring movie, and presenting a project I didn't have time to finish. I wish I was back in second grade and all you had to do was make a Christmas card for your parents. I can so do that.

At least Dillon tried to spice it up at lunch. We don't have an open campus, so we're not allowed to leave at lunch time to go get something to eat. Dillon and I left anyway.

We got cinnamon buns from the closest bakery we were able to find. They were delicious and the goo kept sliding down our chins. Once, Dillon snatched a napkin from the table and wiped it from my chin. I had completely stopped moving and stared at him. He dropped the napkin and scooted a little closer. Then I saw the time behind his head on the wall and we both jumped up and Dillon sped back to school. I didn't get the kiss, but the cinnamon was just as sweet.

We took a test in Mrs. Olden's class. I used a normal pencil and got out of my seat to drop it on her desk. When leaving the classroom, she gave me a small smile and I told her to have a good Christmas break.

May and Ashley met me outside my classroom and we three got in my car and my driver took us directly to my house.

Right now we're sitting in large, cushioned seats in my home theater. We each have our own bowls of popcorn and sodas in a glass cup with ice. Our eyes are glued to the 90inch screen T.V. across from us. I put my feet up on the chair in front of me. Ashley does the same and May brings her legs to her chest.

I hear the door open and close behind us. Jamui comes in and bends down to whisper in my ear.

"Phone call," he said.

"Who?" I asked. Dillon?

"I don't know."

I tell my friends I'll be right back. I follow my brother out of the room and he hands me the phone. I wait until he's done climbing down the stairs before putting the phone to my ear.

"Hello?"

"Hi, Mariam."

Ms. Bell.

"Have you been ignoring my calls and texts?" she asks.

"No. I lost my phone," I admit.

"Oh, I see. Well, I left a voicemail saying I'm visiting tomorrow."

"What for?" I wonder.

"To give you a gift," she answers.

"Did I do something good?"

"You deserve one."

I chew on my upper lip and crack my thumb.

"I guess I'll see you tomorrow," I said.

"I guess you will," she agrees.

May and Ashley sleep over. We stay up until three in the morning in my room with the door locked and movies and candy and boy talk. Lots of boy talk.

We fall asleep without meaning to. We were dog-tired. We then wake up around nine and they leave for home. I fall back on my bed. The moment I close my eyes, dreams and pitch darkness shut me in.

"Do you smell it?"

I look up from where I'm sitting with my legs crossed and my back to a wall. Its dark, no light and nothing to see. I try to uncross my legs but they feel as if they're stuck under cement.

"Do you smell it?"

It's Malcolm West's voice. The question is whispered but loud in my ears.

I can smell it. Blood.

A light turns on in front of me. It's just like a spotlight on a stage. There are two people, one bending over the other. Ike bending over Erika. They're giving me a show.

Ike has a knife in his hand, the blade crimson red and glinting under the light. There's blood on the floor, around, and under my sister's body, in her hair and covering her fingers. He digs the knife in her chest and I try to scream. Ike looks up.

But I see Malcolm's face.

"Do you hear it?"

Now I'm outside. There's a burning heat and I'm in the middle of nowhere. The ground is just a bunch of dirt, the sky an Alice blue. A large tree as tall as a castle appears before me. I step back just to see the top.

"Do you hear it?"

Dr. Jeff. Definitely his voice, no doubt about it.

Then I hear it. Ear-splitting and childlike and dreadful. My sister's scream. My body shudders and my hands turn into fists. I run for the tree and grab the branches, struggling to heave myself up to reach the top. But each one I grab breaks like a twig. I keep tumbling to the ground and at the top, Erika screams and Dr. Jeff laughs.

"Do you see it?"

The ground opens up underneath me. I cry out and fall through. Rocks and bits of grass are dropping below along with me. I grab at the walls, my hands brushing up against weeds that I can't get a hold on and stones that cut through my skin. My clothes are being ripped and scratched and my eyes are getting columns of dirt into them.

"Do you see it?"

Shelly's voice is like raging murmurs. Like there's more than one of her and they're all very displeased with me.

Blinking lights switch on. Just as bulbs would flicker before powering out was how these lights acted. They're trained at the walls. And as I fall, I can see exactly what Shelly wants me to.

There's vines tied to Erika's wrists. Her arms hang loose as Mother Nature holds her up, dangling like a demon watching a sinned being falling towards Hell. Some of the vines have her trapped around the neck and others keep her hanging by her ankles. Each one I pass, her eyes open and mouth slightly agape, I see Shelly's face. Grinning at me with lips as red as clotted blood.

A smile that bellows, "I fooled you".

I open my eyes. They're wet and so is the corner of my pillow. Even though I had not gotten under the covers before my head hit the bed, the sheets are wrinkled. I must've wrestled around. I never had a dream that contained other people instead of Ike and Erika. And Ike wasn't even in this one. The blame was on everyone else *except* him.

Malcolm asked if I smelt the blood and Dr. Jeff wanted to know if I could hear her scream. Shelly was yelling into my ears to know whether or not I can see my sister hanging by evil vines. Most of the time I ignore my dreams, even gotten used to them. Ms. Bell said they're your fears. What part do I fear, Malcolm spilling Erika's blood, Dr. Jeff torturing her, or Shelly suspending her dead body in the air?

What did Ms. Bell tell me to do about the nightmares?

"Take a run," she had said. "Doesn't matter if you like running or hate running. You take a jog and the pumping of your heart and your feet hitting the ground will help you forget. And if it doesn't, run faster."

It's a little past five. I throw on some sweats and a T-shirt. I tie on my shoes and make off onto the street.

After a couple of minutes, I stop running hard and keep it at a steady jog. I'm hot and my ankles hurt, but I don't stop because I can still smell the blood and hear my sister scream and see her hanging in the air. I tried shutting my eyes while I jogged, but that just made it a lot worse.

Maybe Ms. Bell's advice isn't good enough.

"Mariam?"

I turn my head to look behind myself. I see Dillon standing there with one hand in his pocket, matching sweats, and green earphones. His eyes, always so bright and alive, stare at me without a blink.

"Hi-" I say, right before I do the most embarrassing thing I've ever done.

I trip.

There's a crack in the sidewalk in front of me and the tip of my foot totally slams into it, immediately halting my jogging and forcing me to fall face first.

I hit the pavement like a bike dropping sideways. Both my hands fall into the snow, ice digging into my fingernails and freezing my skin in a second. There are hidden rocks and they jump out and scratch my fingers. The skin on my knees burn and the snow creates a wet spot on my sweats. Tears scratch behind my eyes but sniffing shoos them away.

Dillon rushes to my side and drops to his knees.

"Are you okay?"

"I'm fine," I answer. Why did he have to be here to see me do that?

He grins and I think he's about to laugh at me, but then he asks, "Just doing a gravity check?"

I smile, embarrassed beyond imaginable, and let out a weak laugh. "Yeah. I like to check once in a while just to make sure it's right."

Dillon laughs and helps me back onto my feet. I brush off some leafs that stuck to my sweats and massage my cold hands.

"Let me see," says Dillon.

I let him take my hand. He touches the new scratches lightly like an artist gingerly adding clouds to a canvas. Then he turns my hand over and grazes the back with his lips. He gives me a casual glance and I look away, beaming.

Then his smile falls and he drops my hand.

"What happened to your neck?" he questions.

I face him again, shielding the bruises from his view, but he turns my head. He touches them with one finger and I wince. He takes his hand back and I step away from him.

"Who did this to you?" he asks. His eyes begin to dim, a look of worry in them.

"Nothing. No one. I'm fine!" I exclaim, repeating the same words I used on Malcolm. Please don't ask me questions.

"Mariam-"

"I said I'm fine."

Drop it Dillon, I thought.

He stares at me a bit longer before running his hand through his hair and glancing to the side.

"You know I was planning on calling you when I got back home," he confesses.

"Really?" I said. "What for?"

"To ask what you were doing tonight."

"You mean…to ask me on a date?" I slowly ask. I hope I'm not sweating on my forehead and I really hope I don't smell like sweat and I really, *really* hope Dillon can't hear the rapid beating of my heart as I'm literally screaming my head off inside.

He shrugs like ten year old Dillon used to shrug. Then he does one hard nod and clears his throat. "Yes. Yes," he repeats. "I'm asking you out."

I nod. "Okay. I accept."

It begins to drizzle and Dillon steps closer.

"Then I'll see you in two hours?" he asks.

"Great. See you then," an uncontrolled grin forms on my lips.

"And this time, dress casual," he said.

"Awe, no rich restaurant?" I make a pouty face as if I really cared. I'm just glad I'll be with Dillon.

Dillon just smiles and turns to leave.

"I like your hair," Dillon comments.

"Thanks," I say, and smooth it back down once again. Oh God *please*, don't let Ike ruin this date. *Please*.

Once I got home, I jumped into the shower and then rummaged through my drawers and closet looking for that one outfit Dillon will like. I put on a white shirt and dark blue shorts. Under the shorts I stretched on leggings so my legs won't freeze. I throw on a fur coat over my shoulders to keep my arms warm. I straightened my hair twice and stuck in black hoop earrings.

Dillon looks hot. Hair silky, smooth, plain white shirt, black jeans, and a simple gray coat that has no hood. He has on a gold watch and white shoes. And he smells absolutely great.

He parks the car on the side of the road. We're in a less rich area than last time. About the same amount of people and cars are out tonight, and even though it's really cold and there's ice and snow on the ground, the bright lights and happy noise is beautiful.

We both climb out of his car and he wraps his arm around my shoulder. But this time he does it a little different. He does it like we're a couple. We walk for a few minutes on the sidewalk, turning a corner and crossing a street. Then we stop at a place and Dillon holds the door open for me.

Inside, the scent of pizza runs up into my nose. The place is crowded. Kids are jumping around and running in and out of the arcade beside the bathroom. The walls are painted white and red. The floor is dark brown. Multiple fans hang from the ceiling.

We find a seat that we like, giving us a view of the business outside. A waiter with a red ring poking out of her tongue takes our order. A medium size pizza, one half barbecue (Dillon), the other half Hawaiian (me).

My feet kick Dillon's booth for fun. I stare out the window at the cars driving and the crazy citizens outside trying to get to one place and another.

When Dillon and I were young, our parents would take us here all the time. We would stuff the pizza into our mouths and run into the arcade. Dillon would play this game were you had to kill all these disgusting zombies and I would play Pac-man, staring at the screen unblinking until I cried. When we lost all our coins on the same games, we would beg our mom's for a dollar or two. Like all mothers, they would say no at first, we'd give them the puppy dog face and, defeated, they'd give us each a dollar. We'd use it up in a second and beg and beg until our mom's wallets were empty. They'd try to make us feel guilty that we spent all their money, though it never worked. We were too happy to feel guilty.

That's the way it went when we were in elementary every other Friday. It stopped when Dillon ignored me in first period and wouldn't sit with me at lunch. He would sit with them, flirting with Nelci. At first, when I saw him sitting with them, I thought I was dreaming. But when I didn't wake up, I knew it was reality.

Then I looked at the next table beside me and watched Ashley laughing when May's milk had spilled over the front of her shirt. Ashley saw me staring and waves me over. I sat by them and we begin laughing at how we we're partners in getting in trouble in first and second grade. I came to their table every day, and after that, Dillon was thrown to the back of my mind.

I clinch my fist.

It's just about one of the worst feelings in the world when you lose your best friend, especially if they're also your secret crush.

And for a while, I thought *I* was the one who had down something wrong.

Calm down, Mariam, I think. I open my hand and lay it against the table.

It's different now. He said he missed me. He was scared to talk to me because he didn't know if I would take him back. Truth is, I would take him back even if he asked for forgiveness thirty years later. He's my best friend no matter what.

Our pizzas come and we grab the one we want. Dillon eats quickly, looking like he swallows right when the pizza hits his mouth. I take small bites only because I'm not that hungry.

"You remember Lucky?" Dillon suddenly asks when he finishes his second slice.

I light up. "How could I forget?"

Lucky was a baby poodle me and Dillon found when we were in fourth grade. We found it behind a rosebush with a broken leg. I wrapped the leg with some of my mom's supplies. Every day after school, me and Dillon would go to the dog and feed it food and water. We never told our parents about Lucky because we knew we'd get in trouble.

One day when we went back to the rosebush to check on him, we found him gone. We searched and searched, calling out his him. But we never found him. I wonder where that dog is now.

"He favored you," Dillon talks. "But most people favor you over me."

I shake my head, but I couldn't help myself from smiling. "That's not true."

"Yes it is. Teachers, old people, dogs, kids, even my grandma likes you more than me."

"What about Nelci and your other friends?" I ask.

"You mean my *old* friends? Don't worry, I'm sure if they actually knew you, they would forget me. And Nelci doesn't really like anybody. She's pathetic," he said.

"Is cute Dillon disappointed his crush didn't turn out the way he wanted her to?"

"Yes," he nods, "cute Dillon is a little disappointed."
I laugh.

"What about your crush?" he wonders.

"What about him?"

"Did he turn out the way you wanted him to?"

"I don't know. Did you Dillon?"

He grins and I smile. Then I begin to laugh and I cover my mouth with my hand to stop from laughing so hard, but drop it after I realize that it's not working. It accidentally falls on top of Dillon's. I leave it there as if I didn't notice. He pretends not to notice too.

I finish two more pizzas with one hand and he does the same. When we're full, we take a step towards the arcade but think better of it. Instead, we leave the restaurant and enter the noise of traffic and talking.

"It's a nice night," I notice. "Let's walk around."

He offers me his arm and I twine mine through it. We turn the opposite direction of the way to the car, entering the mass crowds of shopaholics, party-animals, and fresh couples.

With our bodies close, walking over ice and snow and speaking in low voices, we laugh about our past. The pranks we used to do to Dillon's older sister or how we'd race up a tree to see who's faster. My dad's best friend owns a candy store and he'd let us come in and take as much as we'd like. Of course I ran for the chocolate and Dillon loved anything that took you forever to chew and swallow. Once we pretended we we're camping out in a dangerous forest, but all we did was put up a tent in my backyard and Jamui would come outside at random times and shake the tent like a wild beast.

I think of taking his hand. Just grabbing it and squeezing our fingers together. I'm so close I can smell both the aftershave and cologne. I can see his smile lines that lead to his lips and I tighten the hold on his arm.

He looks at me and smiles and for a moment I think I'm about to get a certain wish granted.

Then a couple walks out of a door and almost runs into us. Dillon and I stop in time and the couple seems not to notice us at all. The man has a bottle in his hand with the other one hanging on the girls shoulder. The girl is hardly wearing anything, just shorts, a T-shirt, and white boots. She must be freezing.

We step aside for the two of them. They laugh loud like everything around them is a joke and they hold on to one another as if the other person is a crutch. The guy takes one last swing of the beer, almost choking on the little bit left, and drops it behind him.

"Crazy old lady!" he calls back at the closing door. The girl laughs and tries to jump up and kiss his cheek but trips, catching his arm to keep her balance.

They cross the street. Dillon looks up at the blue lit up sign over the door. **Fortuneteller**.

I release his arm and he takes my wrist.

"Come on," he urges

He opens the door and pulls us both in.

Inside, the room is dark and alive with smells. There are candles instead of lights and long tables against the wall with green and light blue spheres. Trinkets scatter a brown, old desk, and a fan set on the floor has its wings turning so slow, not a beat of wind is coming from it. We follow the claret rug to the back of the room, moving through a short hallway with silver boarded mirrors hanging on each side. I can see my hard cheekbones and the point of Dillon's adorable nose.

Once we hit the back of the building, finally stepping off the rug, all I can smell is jasmine. Lots of it as I try not to cough and breathe through my nose. Dillon looks as if to have the same problem when he scrunches up his nose and squints like the smell is burning his eyes.

Before us is a round table with a red silk as a tablecloth. Two thin candles in the middle of the table. The candles are set on each side of one glass crystal ball mounted on a stand. It's about as big as my head and basically looks like a huge marble. There are three padded chairs and sitting in one of them is an old lady with curly gray hair and pale blue eyes. There's about twenty bracelets on each of her arms and ten necklaces. There are three holes in both ears and an earring takes up each spot.

She looks up when we enter.

"How may I help you?" she asks, with a young voice that sounds awkward with her elderly look.

Dillon points his head at me. "She'd like her fortune told."

I give him a look. I don't remember saying that. Dillon just smiles and shrugs.

The woman lifts her left arm to point at a basket on a table by a picture frame of a huge eyeball. There are a couple of old five dollar bills and quarters already in there but nowhere near filling the basket. Dillon takes out his wallet and adds more.

"Take a seat," commands the fortuneteller.

We take the two seats across from her. She lays her eyes on me and I suddenly grow cold.

"Why have you sought me out?" the woman questions.

What do fortunetellers do? They tell you your future or past or answer questions. Well, my past isn't very bright and the only question I have is whether or not Dillon will kiss me goodnight. The future is what I'm not sure about.

"Tell me my future," I answer.

The fortuneteller cracks her neck. She raises her hands above the crystal ball and mist like fog immediately appears. It clouds the whole ball, shielding our views like a black cape. Like Ike's black cape.

"I see…I see darkness," the lady speaks. "I see sorrow and black. A woman and two men."

I hold my breath.

"There's fright," she goes on. She slowly turns her hands around the ball. A red smoke forms in the middle, dancing around the darkness. "I see trees and snow. And anger."

"Anger?" I choke. "Who's angry?"

She doesn't answer. I think about repeating my question until the crystal ball lights up. It's amazingly bright and Dillon and I both look away while the lady stares with eyes wide open. The brightness dies down and I look closely into the ball. Red on the left and blue on the right squirt out and mashes into each other. The color purple blossoms from the middle, filling the whole ball in a swirling motion.

Well, I've never seen anything like that before.

The fortuneteller leans her head back. Her eyes trail up to my face. The eyes look even paler, but still and all look mad and confused.

"What are you?" she mutters to me.

"What?" I say.

"You're not normal. What is that in your head? What is it?"

"Please-" I try.

"What have you've done? What are you? What is it!" she demands, slamming both her fists down, shaking the table.

"I think we should leave," I suggest. "Dillon?"

I look over at him. His eyes are trapped on the crystal ball as the purple grows darker. A lilac to a violet to a plum color. It's beautiful really, but then ugly when you look too close. My future: beautiful, until you go inside and find the secrets and locked doors.

I jump from my chair and grab Dillon's hand, oblivious to the fact that are fingers squeeze together like I wanted it to, and pull him out of his seat. He follows as if in a daze. Behind us, she still asks me 'what is it' and mutters, as if obvious, 'I'm not normal'.

I'm not normal. I'm not.

I break through the door.

Fresh air has never smelt better. No more jasmine and the sight of rainbow spheres or the color lilac or violet or plum. I unloose Dillon's hand to rub my eyes and groan in my palm.

"What the heck just happened?" asks Dillon. He looks a little star-struck, with his eyes on me, accusingly.

"That lady," I explain, feeling out of breath, "she's crazy. You know fortunetellers randomly pick which trick to do on the next customer."

"It didn't feel like a trick," he said.

"So then you believe her? You think I'm not normal?"

I know I just threw him in a rocky situation, but I don't care. I really like him. I need to know what he thinks of me so I'll be sure on what page he's on.

"I never said that. What I think is that you haven't been telling me the truth. How did you get those bruises?" he asks, once again.

I groan. "This again? I said I'm fine."

"Yeah, I know you said you were fine. You said it twice. But that doesn't make me believe you."

I focus on his face. His eyes like a heavenly light and staring at me without looking away. I bite my upper lip, hiding the truth in so tight, I bleed. And Dillon waits, watching me and hoping…

"You don't trust me," he concludes, as if reality has just sunk in.

"No, Dillon. I do trust you," I say, not one single lie leaving my mouth. "I just…I just…"

"You just *don't trust me*," he says stronger with his shoulders stiff. "I guess this date isn't going to end exactly the way I wanted it to."

"It's my fault," I said.

"No, it's my fault. I shouldn't have rushed this- rushed you. You're obviously not ready to do something more about our relationship," he steps back.

"Dillon-" I said.

"And here I am thinking that this would be the date that changes everything. That there might possibly be a kiss this time. But I see now this date has only changed what I thought."

I cross my arms as he keeps going on. He did this as a kid also. When he really needed to let something out, he'd babble on and on until he let it go. He'd talk over you if you tried to speak. Something miraculous was only able to make him shut-up.

I stride to Dillon and grab his face and gently force his head towards mine. I press our lips together. He swallows his words and I lean in closer, feeling his hair in my fingers and the tickle from his eyelashes when he closes them. Slowly, he wraps his arms around my waist, holding me against his hard chest and kissing me back intensely. I think I bite his lip once, but I'm not completely sure. I can taste barbecue pizza when we open our mouth wider and my body feels as if I'm on the top of the world.

I break away first, releasing his face and pulling my head away. He still holds me with one hand, unwilling to let me go. He opens his eyes and a little smile grows on his lips with the nonpareil color in his eyes shining like a star.

"Who would've thought my best friend would be a good kisser," he says. He leans in.

"It's getting late," I said, stopping him.

"Did your parents expect you home at a certain time?"

And then I remember.

My eyes lighten up from the realization and I jump out of Dillon's tough arms. "Ms. Bell! I totally forgot."

Dillon drops his arms. "Who?"

"My tutor. I need to get home."

"You have a tutor?"

"*Dillon.*"

"Ok, fine. But I'm pretty sure kissing me would be a lot more fun. But, hey it's cool, everyone has their own opinion."

He takes my hand and pulls me in the right direction to his car.

"When's the next time I'm going to see you?" Dillon asks as he turns off his car parked in front of my house. The lights are all out. But a familiar car is parked in the driveway beside us. Ms. Bell waited for me this whole time? She must be pissed.

I shrug. Really, I wanted to ask the next time I'm going to be able to kiss him again. But, yeah right am I going to embarrass myself by asking him that. I still can't believe that I grabbed him and forced my lips on his.

"Is it soon?"

"I hope so," I tell.

He grins brightly. "So, I'll call you?"

I grin also. "Yeah, call me."

"Ok. Good night, Mariam," and he leans over and kisses me on the cheek.

I climb out of the car. I step back and watch him pull out. He gives a wave and a wink before driving off. The last thing I see is the back of his corvette and the sound of its reverberate engine.

Across the street is a black truck. One of Malcolm's men, I suppose. For some reason, it feels good that Malcolm said he was going to do something, and actually does it. Even if it was against my wishes.

I unlock the front door. I have no idea where my family is. It's almost past midnight; they should be home by now. I mean, if my family isn't home, then how else did Ms. Bell get in?

I enter my house and shut the door behind me. There's a light on in the kitchen. It's the only light we leave on when we go to sleep. Only, no one's home except Ms. Bell. I step inside the kitchen to find it empty. I begin to worry.

I'm given the feeling you get in your gut when you know that something's wrong and you automatically begin to panic. Sweat breaks out on my forehead and my senses sharpen. The house is too quiet. The air feels heavy and sated with fear. I put my hands in fists to keep them from trembling.

I move toward the stairs. They look so big and long like I'm three all over again. I hit the first step. Then the second one and the third. The fourth creaks loudly under my foot and I freeze. Silence.

I look up on the second floor. I can't see anything in the dark hallways. I can't hear anything either. It doesn't exactly make me feel any better. I still have no clue if I'm alone or with hiding visitors. But I keep going slowly, but quick enough not to be too frightened by the darkness surrounding me and blinding me.

I smell it before I see it. A hard iron smell and a little sourly sweet. I know the smell of blood when it enters my nose. At the top of the staircase there's a lump on the ground in the shape of a human. A human not moving.

I stare first. I'm not those types of people that do without thinking. What if Ike wants me to run to the body? What if it is Ike, pretending to be dead?

And what if that's Ms. Bell, says that really annoying part in your brain that always seems to be right. But the thought did have me running.

I drop to my knees by the stock-still body and turn it on its back. In the dark I can see the white mustache and lifeless eyes staring up into nowhere. A badge gleams, reacting when the moon hits it. Something drips onto my fingers and I take my hand back. There's blood spilling from his chest and sinking into the carpet. At least it's not Ms. Bell, right? At least she's fine.

Until I see another body. One more cop, slumped against the wall with his head down and his gun hanging loose in his right hand. He's drooling blood and his left ankle is turned the opposite way. I look away, fear rushing through my head. I forget the cops and run to my closed bedroom door with nothing stopping me.

I slam my door open and flick on the light.

On the floor in front of my bed, Ms. Bell is sprawled on the ground. Not moving. I'm not sure if she's even breathing.

I drop onto my hands and knees and crawl myself over to her slack body. I hold her hand. It's cold. Desperate, I check for a pulse and a heartbeat. Nothing. I check again but I get no new response from the inside of her body. I even whisper her name, but of course, she doesn't answer.

"No!" I scream, anger rising in me. "Ms. Bell, please!"

I shake her body hard. Her dead body. I squeeze her hand so tight I make her bones crack.

"No, not now. Please, not now," I beg to no one. "Don't leave me…"

It's over. She's as alive as a rock. I move her hair out of her face and find ugly, purple bruises on her throat. That's what he did. He choked her to death. He brought his hands around her throat and strangled the life out of her. She had done nothing to him and she should've never died this way. This is my entire fault. I was making out with a boy while people we're being murdered in my own home.

I wipe at the tears with my free hand, contending to hold them back, but who cares. No one's here to watch me cry and the one person able to tell me how to deal with the tears will never speak again. I think of her delightful and stunning personality and I cry harder.

I drop her hand and get back on my feet. A white note is stuck to my mirror. I squint to read it. Just four words: **come and get me**.

My air gets caught in my throat. Calm down Mariam. I breathe slowly.

I look down at a wrapped present resting on my bed.

'I'm visiting tomorrow to give you a gift. You deserve one.'

I pull at the dark blue wrapping. With the wrapping cleared away, a square box lays on the bed. I flip open the lid.

A blue scarf is rolled up at the bottom of the box. I smooth my fingers over the fabric. It's soft and silky. And sticking out from the middle of the scarf is a bottle of that blue liquid. Just what I needed.

I survey the taunting note on my mirror. I can just about see Ike smiling through the paper or see the wind slapping his coat around in the air. I can hear his laugh, loud like Santa Clause's and evil like a mad scientist. I touch the bruises on my neck and I figure out exactly what I should do.

Before picking up the home phone, I search the rest of the house. I need to make sure that my family is definitely someplace else. I can't see why Ike would want to hurt them. I still can't see why it had to be Ms. Bell and how he knew where she'd be. If all he wanted was my attention, he damn well has it.

I punch in the seven digits. He answers immediately, sounding wide awake and irked.

"I don't understand why teenagers need cellphones so bad when they don't ever answer the phone," he whines from the other end. I ignore Malcolm's tone, set the phone on speaker, and rip off my shorts and leggings.

"Lost my phone," is all I say.

"Do you know how many times I called you? Your watchdog had no idea where you went and you weren't at home because Ms. Bell kept ringing the doorbell. No one was home-"

"Ms. Bell's dead," I reveal. I bite my lip as fresh tears burst. I pull on jeans and throw a sweater over my shirt. "She's *dead.*"

"No," he mutters. It's too much for him to believe. "No, I just spoke to her a couple of hours ago. I just spoke to her *and* her guards."

"They're dead too."

"This can't be."

"He killed them in my house," I said. My hands tremble. "Why Ms. Bell? Why did it have to be Ms. Bell?"

"Mariam, I need you to calm down and stay where you are," he said.

"That's not going to happen," I dry my face. "I'm taking a Charmaine Robinson's car and going straight to his place."

I know he doesn't know who Charmaine is, but he can look her up in a hot second. That's the point.

"Mariam, *stop*. You're not thinking straight," he tries.

"I'm thinking fine." I tie on my running shoes and tug on a jacket.

"He will *kill* you."

"Not if I kill him first."

I end the call and snatch the blue medicine out of the box. This is just about the best present I have ever gotten. I peer down at Ms. Bell. Ike *will* pay for this.

I leave my house in a jog, passing my watchdog that's hunched over in his seat with his eyes blankly staring at his lap. I forget the image and pick up my speed.

If Ike wants me to come and get him, that's exactly what I'm going to do.

CHAPTER 18

I end up in front of Charmaine's house after a mile of running. Breathing hard, I jog up her porch and bang on her door. She doesn't answer quickly enough so I bang even harder and stab the doorbell with my finger.

"Who is it?" I hear her voice, her footsteps growing closer and closer.

"The Big Bad Wolf," I answer, sarcastically. "Open up!"

She does and she's poking out her lips in a smirk. "That's not how it goes. He actually says-"

"Yeah, yeah a huff and a puff. I need to use the car," I tell her, stepping into the house.

"I don't know, my boyfriend was thinking of taking me out."

"First off, it's almost one in the morning. Where the heck will you guys go? And second, it's an emergency, Charmaine. It will only take a few hours."

"Hours-" she begins, but stops and looks at me curiously. "Are you going back to that party I had to pick you up from?"

I clear my throat. "Yes, that's exactly it."

Charmaine smiles. "I guess you could use the car," she shrugs and pulls one key out of her pocket. She tosses it into my hand. "Bring the car back in one piece. If you get drunk, please have somebody who isn't as wasted as you to drive you home. You have until seven in the morning. Call me if anything goes wrong," she orders.

"I will Mom."

She rolls her eyes. "And just for the record, there are clubs open right now waiting for me and my boyfriend, because the real fun doesn't start until we get there."

"And just for *your* record, there will be some cops stopping at your house to find out my whereabouts. Tell them everything," I said.

"Wait, what?"

I drop down from the porch with the key and climb inside the red truck parked in the driveway. I start the car, roll of onto the street, and follow the directions placed in my head, leaving Charmaine with her mouth open.

It's time Ike finds out who he's dealing with.

I try not to, but I cry the whole way to Ike's warehouse. The loss of Ms. Bell hurt me a little more than I wanted it to. The tears fall like a water hose. I think half of the reason I'm crying is because Ike killed another innocent person because he was jealous, thought they were a threat, or because he was mad. Specifically mad at me.

But it hurt even more to know that he killed her only to get my attention. That bastard.

I leave the truck in the empty gas station; one that I'm starting to realize is pretty abandoned. I leave the key hanging from the lock on the outside of the door, so that if anything happens to me, Charmaine's boyfriend will still have his car.

I walk at my regular pace. There's no need to walk faster or slower- he already knows I'm coming.

I can see the dark warehouse up ahead when the wind decides to pick up. The weather in New York sucks the most when it's around Christmas. It starts to sprinkle a little, the water weighing down my eyelashes. I blink them away and hug myself, dragging my feet through the snow and making sure not to trip on the ice.

I circle around the warehouse until I find the door I used to escape. Hesitantly, I try the handle. It opens. I close my eyes and bite my lip as the door makes several major creaks when I push it more open. I slide inside when I have enough room.

Around me, and at the bottom of the staircase, is pitch black. I slowly walk down each step. I almost scream when the door behind me slams shut by the wind outside. I clutch at my heart and proceed down the staircase. Every movement I make has the staircase creak even more. I breathe in a relaxed motion. I know I can do this.

Finally, I'm at the bottom and step off the stairs. I retrace my steps. I walk through the hallway, my steps echoing off the walls. The walls are plain and dirty. The ceiling's blank with no lights or anything. There are no windows except for one across the hall, too small for my shoulders to fit through.

I find a closed door. I press my ear against it to listen for a sign that someone's inside. I can't hear anything but a beeping noise coming from the next room. I press my ear against that door.

The beeping keeps going at a steady pace, sometimes going faster and slowing down. It reminds me of a heartbeat. I twist the knob but do not push the door open. It turns all the way.

I shove the door open.

No people. No Ike.

A computer is sitting on a dark brown wooden desk to my left. It's beeping and a bunch of things are popping up on the screen. I shut the door and move to the computer, the sound grabbing my attention. I bend over to check the screen.

It shows a list. A list of names. Some of the names are in blue, others in red. A date and time appears next to the name. I think its children, and the date and time is when they were born. Even their parents' names and where they live shows up. Each beep brings a new name. Each name is either blue or red. Each color meant something. But what?

Beside the computer is a red notebook. I flip it open to the first page. The page is filled with names. Most names are crossed out with a red pen. I read them. None sound familiar. I turn the page.

More names. More names crossed out than on the first page. Right in the middle, is a name I recognize, one not yet crossed out.

Katie Gold.

Katie.

Katie.

I hold my breath and think. Is it her? Is it the little girl I saw in Cold & Good? The one who no more has a grandma and was told to kill me? Are all these names kids with the gift? And the ones crossed out, are they…already dead?

I close my eyes and slowly reopen them. Under Katie Gold's name is Jabari Alexander, Billy Stone, Annie Jones, and so on. Billy's name is crossed out. He must be dead.

I look down the page, a tear wanting to come out of my eyes each time I see a red line over a little boy or girl's name. I turn the page.

The first word at the top of the page is Davy Newton. Name crossed out. And under that, also crossed out with that bloody red ink, is the name Erika-

A door slams shut outside the room I'm in. My eyes peel away from my baby sister's name. I stare at the door. Footsteps walk closer. I hold my breath. The computer keeps beeping and I kind of want it to shut-up, just in case Ike gets curious and comes in to look up a certain name. The footsteps are coming nearer and nearer. I search for a hiding place. There is none.

I'm toast, I think.

But I hear the footsteps proceed pass the door. I began to breathe naturally again. Soon, the footsteps disappear down the hallway.

I look back down at the notebook with all the names of kids that died and will. Unless I do something about it. I stare at the beeping computer filling in more kids. Babies. There are more blue names popping up than red. My guess is the red are the special ones. There's so many of them. I wonder if he just randomly picks a name and seeks out their information.

I've had enough, I think. I close the notebook and put the computer behind me as I go back to the door that I entered. I first listen for footsteps. There are none, but just to be sure, I calm my quaking heart and feel the knife transform into my right hand. I open the door and step out.

Almost immediately, a foot connects to my jaw and I go crashing to the dirty ground. A kick to the stomach makes me cough and clutch my chest. But I keep my brain on my knife, gripping it hard enough to indent the shape into my palm. I'm dragged onto my feet by strong hands. I shut my eyes. He pushes my body against the wall with such force that I was close to blacking out.

"Open your eyes!" he screams, spit flying all over my face.

I peak. But my eyes close tightly at the fear of seeing his anger.

I feel the razor-sharp blade with my finger.

"I said open your eyes, dammit!" he yells again.

I do as he says. It's not a pretty sight.

Forget the way his brown eyes are glaring at me with such venom that it could make a pro-wrestler walk away. Don't even care about the red, snarling face above me. It's the burn marks, the burn marks I put on him, that's just about making me want to pee in my pants. Ugly and red and dark. All over his face. Some skin is gone under his chin and above his left eyebrow. You can almost see bone and I feel like upchucking. I aimed the fire at his chest, I know I did. I guess it just decided to journey a little higher, and now Ike's face is nothing but a burnt surface. I know if I touch it, I'd feel something rough and harsh under my fingers. If I looked like that, I would slice my face off.

I guess I can see why he's pretty mad at me.

He grins a horrifying grin. "Did you like my little present I left in your bedroom?"

I don't cry. I suck in my tears and hold my knife behind my back. "How did you know where she'd be?"

He holds up my cellphone with one hand. "You left something."

I growl. He tosses the phone to the side and it smashes into the wall and breaks into pieces. His hands reach for my throat and I push away my second thoughts as I lodge the knife into his shoulder. It digs in like it was born to be connected to his body.

Ike screams like a girl at the pain. He stares at me unbelievably. His hands move away from me as they grab the blades handle. He begins to try to pull it out of his shoulder, groaning and crying out curses. He's blocking the exit. I run the other way, my brain thinking of only that blade in his shoulder.

Of course, I'm so frightened that I lose my concentration and I feel the blade disappear.

I find a random door and slam it open. I run into a room with an old bed that has no covers. There's a T.V. box and a brown couch set in front of it. I hide behind the side of the couch that's not facing the door. I balance on my knees and listen.

His heavy breathing comes before his body does. I hold my breath as he bounds into the room, eyes looking around wildly. Too soon he finds me. A large ball of fire punches me in my chest and I trip onto the floor. I slap at the flames on my shirt, singeing my jacket and burning into my skin. I scream. I fall onto my stomach, praying that the weight will extinguish the fire.

"You like that?" Ike shouts over me. "I don't think you do."

Of course I don't, you piece of crap! I want to shout at him. I try to calm down to think. I can do this.

Size: no size, no shape. Color: clear. Touch: wet. I think of Ike's body, where he's standing, what's over him and what's around him. My whole body feels damp, and then it's gone and the fire keeps eating through my shirt.

The water comes from behind Ike and on his sides. It attacks him with a loud splash, some of the water sprinkling on me. The water hits his face, his whole body. The fire on me dies with a light, including the pain. Ike falls onto his knees as the water tries to choke him and just simply drown him, moving and jumping like its human. I try to hold my strength on it, only I feel like fainting. All I want to do is sleep. Sleep sounds really good right now. I throw the water away in an invisible pond.

I start crawling for the door. His nails scratch against my skin as he grabs my right ankle. I scream at the sudden touch and twist around. I bring my left leg up to my chest and smack a kick in his jaw. His hand lets go of my ankle. I climb onto my feet. He grabs the hood of my jacket, forcing me back. The jacket slips off my arms and I smack my hand right across his cheek, even harder than when he did it to me three months ago. Scared out of my life, I start running.

I sprint out the room. I race through the hallways and up the stairs, shoving open the door. I dash across the street and enter the woods.

It's pouring rain. The grass is covered with dirty snow and ice and the wind is blowing in all directions. The rain goes at my clothes and face, gluing my shirt to my skin. Trees are spread out all around me. They're too high, high enough to block out the moon. Actually, I can't see anything. But I keep running deeper and deeper into the woods. The deeper I go the darker it gets. The deeper I go, the quieter it gets. The deeper I go, the more I get lost.

I stop running. I struggle to breathe calmer. I search around. I can't see anything.

And then I hear my name.

"Mariam…"

My breath stops. My heart kind of wants to too.

"Mariam."

I step back. The voice is close. His voice.

"Mariam, watch out!" he shouts behind me.

I jump and turn around. Where is he? Oh my gosh, where is he?

"Where are you?" I even whisper to the trees.

"Let's play hide and seek," he suggests. Still no sigh of him. I can't even tell where his voice is coming from anymore. Now it's just bouncing off the trees.

"Let's not," I say.

"Great, I'll count to ten."

"No," I mutter with large fright.

"One…two…"

"No!"

"Three…four…"

I start to run forward, more deep into the woods. But his voice is *everywhere*.

"Five…"

I sprint past trees. Branches grab at my hair. I jump over logs. Snow and rain soaks my socks.

"Six…"

I pull myself through two close trees. My heart beats faster. My feet don't stop moving forward.

"Seven…eight…" his voice rings through my ears. "Better run faster."

That's all I'm thinking. Run faster. Run faster. Except I have no idea where I'm going. I have no idea what's going to happen after he's done counting. I don't want to find out.

"Nine…"

No. No. No.

"Ten. Ready or not, here I come," he chuckles.

Out of nowhere, a tree gets in my way and I smash right into it. I fall on the ground and moan at the pain in my forehead. I start crawling. The tree's gone. Of course it is.

I need strength, I think. Strength.

I reach into my pocket. I feel the glass in my fingers. I take out the bottle and unscrew the cap. I can hear him. His heavy breathing, his feet beating against the ground. I put the bottle to my wet lips and plug my nose. I chug it all.

The glass bottle is dropped out of my hands as Ike slams into me. We both fall on the floor. There's no grass- just water, ice, and snow. The snow sinks into my clothes, dousing my jeans and the water runs down my shirt.

Ike socks me in the face. Blood trickles out of my nose. He punches me again, one that forces my teeth to stab themselves into my tongue. Blood fills my mouth. I can feel the medicine trying to reach my brain, give it more power, but the punches are knocking it back down. If only he would stop hitting me for more than five seconds.

Ike hops onto his feet and pulls me up by the hair. Strands rip out I think. But I'm not sure I'm feeling anything right now. Basically, my whole body feels like its burning. Every bone and muscle hurts and there's blood running down my face.

He shoves me against a big tree. The branches cut into my cheeks. My arms stay frozen at my sides. I can't even feel them anymore. My legs want to crumble to the ground but Ike keeps me standing, body leaned against the tree, his hands pushing my shoulders back.

Ike sinks his face in closer, his dreadful breath swimming up my nose. Water from the rain runs down his face, dripping off the tip of his chin.

"See what you do? I just kill the kids, never torture," he says. "But you're making it very difficult, Mariam."

I close my eyes, I can feel it, the medicine rising up and up, trying to find the part in my brain that makes me think stronger.

"Just like your sister, huh?" he continues. His lips come so near to mine. To the one's Dillon had kissed. To the one's he might never ever kiss again. "With all that screaming and fighting she was doing."

I feel the medicine grope through my brain. I know it's getting closer.

"And then how stupid I was to hit you with that car and crack your head open," he said. "I never really killed her, you know. All I did was give her over to you. She's in you. What's in your head is her."

He moves his lips over to my ear, the air coming from his mouth tickling me. "So when I kill you, I get to kill her all over again."

The medicine hits a powerful nerve. Immediately, I think.

Size: long, skinny. Color: brown. Touch: wood, rough, sharp at one end. Smell: wood.

I suck in my breath. "You're not killing anyone today."

I aim my ruler directly in Ike's throat.

And he catches it right before it hits his skin. My eyes are large as he twirls it in his hand. There's a smile on his lips.

"Nice try," he praises. "But I can see when you think. And you're goanna have to be a little better than that."

I spit in his face. There's blood on my teeth and skating down my bottom lip. "When you die, you'll go straight to Hell." He shrugs, pushing me harder into the tree. The bark pokes through my shirt. "Probably. But not today."

He throws the ruler back and over his head. Before hitting the floor, a mass of light seizes it in its grasp. A weapon appears in Ike's hand; a knife with a six inch handle and the blade going from my wrist to my elbow. I struggle under his hold. He edges the blade under my chin, the cold metal licking my throat.

"I'm going to kill you," he announces. "Slowly. Painfully. It won't be as quick as your sister or your dear old therapist's death. I want you to feel yourself die. I want you to choke on your blood and watch me wash my hands with it."

I pull at his fingers, the ones holding my back against the tree. I try not to move my head too much, as to not have the blade cut into my skin even though it's about to happen now and I will suffer a nasty death.

Ike leans in closer, ready to slice my life in half.

"Drop the weapon and put your hands up."

I glance behind Ike for the voice. He stops moving. Shelly comes from around a tree. In her hand is a handgun, finger on the trigger and arms out. Still, Ike keeps his back to her while Shelly's gun is pointed at his head.

"I said drop the weapon," She commands. "Now!"

Ike works his jaw, contemplating. Then he grins, takes his hand off of me, and twists around to face the agent.

"Drop the weapon."

"You won't shoot me," he says. I watch his finger graze over the blade. The knife cuts through and the wound drips and drips.

Shelly takes two steps forward. Her hair is wet and her coat is soaked through. She has on snow boots and they're covered in snow. "I dare you to test me. Now put the goddam knife down."

The knife disappears.

"Hands up!"

Ike's hands go in the air.

"Shelly!"

Malcolm appears racing through the trees. He stops beside Shelly and makes eye contact with Ike. In one quick motion, his arms are up with a gun between him and the murderer.

Ike drops his hands like he's tired of holding them up and not like as if there's two guns trained on him.

"Put your hands back up-" Shelly orders.

"Awe, isn't this cute," says Ike. "You two are together trying to kill someone."

"Shut-up!" demands Malcolm.

"I'm very impressed by you two. By your lies Shelly and your tricks Malcolm. But you shouldn't have saved her in that basement."

"How do you know about that?" asks Shelly. She's ignoring the rain falling down on her and the messy hair in her face.

Ike smiles. "I have my ways." He turns to Malcolm. "You were supposed to let her die. She was supposed to die there. Why would you save someone that obviously made so much little to you?"

"Stop!" shouts Shelly while Malcolm just stares straight at Ike.

"Risking your life for someone you don't care about?" continues Ike. "You're too sweet."

"I'm only going to tell you *one* more time," speaks Shelly. Her voice is as cold as ice and her blue and green eyes are flaming with odium. "*Put. Your. Hands. Up.*"

"As you wish," and he does exactly what she said, hands back up, completely unarmed. Far behind Shelly and Malcolm you can hear shouting and yelling. Dogs are barking and there are flashlights moving through the trees. More help, if only they would hurry up.

Ike's back to Malcolm. "This is your chance. This is your chance to fix what you screwed up. To give Death what he came for."

He looks at Shelly, pretending her gun is nothing but one made out of paper. "You."

Like a flash, Ike does a whirl with his hand and a handgun appears in his grasp. Just a normal black one with a white slide and brown grip. He aims it at Shelly and her eyes go wide.

"No!" Malcolm cries and charges towards her.

He pulls the trigger just as Malcolm tackles the agent to the ground.

"No!" I scream and struggle to maneuver around Ike. But he reaches out and catches me at the throat, slamming my head against the tree and locking my arms behind me. I battle for air and kick with my feet.

On the ground, Shelly climbs back up and hurries to Malcolm's body on the floor. Not moving, with his head turned to the side and rain and snow covering his face. She holds his head in her hands and rubs his cheeks, calling out his name like he'll answer.

"Ready to die?" Ike asks.

"Why? Why are you doing this?" I want to know. "I've never done anything to you."

He growls. "Yes you have. You possess the same thing I do!"

"So?" I squint to see him through the rain and tears filling my eyes because of the pain.

"So it's mine. I've never had anything. Never! And once, when I discovered what I can do and how it made me special, I had to make sure no one else has it."

"That's selfish! This gift is around the world."

"I know. Which makes me a very busy man. And for the ones that get in my way," he indicates to the two people on the ground behind him, one crying and the other dying, "well, you can see what I do to them."

I bring my knee up, giving him the best kick in the balls I've ever done. I'm let go as he hollers out and drops to the ground.

I swing around and jump over a log. It's probably a bad idea to run away from the direction of the cops that are racing to help, but I know Ike won't follow me if I go that way. And I have a plan. If my plan doesn't work, than I have no theory on how to stop him.

I hear him darting after me and so soon he grabs my arm and twists me around. I trip and fall on my back and he goes down with me. There's a knife in his hand and I take my first strike.

I get my fist right in his head. It hurts, but I think it hurts him more. He groans, there's a brilliant light, and the knife is gone. I shove him off of me and start running again. He chases me and slams me into a tree. I pick up a rock and hit him on the side of his face. A long cut opens up and blood flows down his face. He sneers at me and creates a knife. I slam the rock into his gut and he chokes and falls. I drop the rock and jump over him so he can see the direction I run. He hops onto his feet and sprints after me.

It's a little harder to find a hiding spot on this side of the woods. There's not as much trees and the moon seems to have gotten a lot bigger. But I run myself towards the darkest part of the woods and dive into a clump of bushes and shrubs. I bend down low, dipping my knees into the snow. And then I wait, praying I blend in. I hear his panting breath coming closer. I snatch a thick firm stick from beside me. It's more like a broken branch. Once I see the gleaming blade in Ike's hand, I rush towards him. I hit him on the back of his head and his weapon goes away. I hit him again right after, bringing him to his knees. He moans and grabs his head. His right hand is shivering and then his whole body is shaking on the ground; convulsing.

It's working.

Ike finds my legs in front of him and his eyes trail up to my face. He opens his hand and I smack the stick at his head right at the same moment the knife appears. A coruscating light becomes huge, taking over the murderer's blade, and then vanishes while Ike shakes and chokes on his blood.

I drop the stick and step back, staring at him.

He throws up water and blood. Tears are falling out of his eyes, looking red and going down slow like Jell-O. It looks like a sudden earthquake casts out in his body, because he does a terrible shudder and lands hard on his back. He quivers more and blood bubbles up in his nose, acting as snot. And suddenly, the jerking stops and his head falls to the side. Blood pours out of the corners of his mouth, eyes resembling a dead fish. All is hushed.

I tumble to my knees. I can't breathe. I try to concentrate on the noise from the cops still searching for me through the trees and darkness but all I can hear is a ringing sound that's pulling me towards an unknown world. I fight to keep my eyes open, but that world up ahead, locked in my dreams, beholds such beauty and love.

I give up and fall on my side. I gasp for air, my left hand running over the ground as if looking for my imaginary inhaler. There's several lights coming my way and I keep thinking it's a monster. I try to turn away but it's too hard to move my head. So I shut my eyes so not to come face to face with the beast, earning myself a reason to enter that unknown world so wildly gorgeous.

CHAPTER 19

I'm flying. Sadly, not literally. Someone (or something) is carrying me. Voices are everywhere and warm hands are touching me here and there. A loud sound is blaring in my ears. A siren.

The arms drop me. I land on a soft mattress. Something's stuffed in my mouth. Air flows in. It helps my lungs not work so hard. Another thing is stuck to my wrist. A needle stabs my left arm.

I try to force me eyelids open, but it stays in place. I still hear the siren sound loud in my ears. I can hear the voices but I don't know if I'm alive because I can't feel pain.

The medicine from the needle brings me to sleep.

My eyes tug open. A clean, white ceiling blocks the sky from view. I close my hands and open them again. I wiggle my toes. They move under a soft, silky blanket. I smooth my palm over the mattress I'm on. It's not *my* mattress.

I look around the room. A nightstand is on the left side of the bed I'm in. A big machine is on the right side. A string hanging off it is connected to my arm. Some freaky blowy-nose thing is in my nostrils. The machine is beeping the same rate my heart is. It's neither slow nor fast. That's good, right?

Across the room, May, Dillon, and Ashley sit in chairs, their butts half sliding off. Ashley looks completely washed out, her eyes staring out the window. May looks worried. She's blinking down at her hands, picking at the pink polish on her thumb. Dillon has his elbows on his knees, chin resting in his palms. Eyes glaring at the ground.

I pull myself up in a sitting position. My head burns and it feels like I'm twirling in a circle. I snatch out the two tubes stuck in nose. I whimper because I didn't expect it to hurt that much.

All three of them look up at the sound of me.

"Mariam, are you alright?" May asks. She jumps onto her feet and sits on the edge of my bed. She grabs my hand, the one with the wired glued to it.

"W-where am I?" I ask.

"You're in the hospital," Ashley explains as she leaves her seat with Dillon and stands on the other side of the bed. "You've…you've been asleep for more than thirty-two hours."

"Thirty-two hours?" I repeat. "What happened?"

"Apparently you had a fight with a serial killer," Dillon said, looking the other way.

A fight with a serial killer. Ike Henderson. The list of names. Red ink. The woods. Snow and rain and trees. And blood. Malcolm on the floor. Ike on the floor. Both not moving. And lights searching through the trees and shrubs, lights looking for me.

May rubs her thumb across the back of my hand. Her hold tightens a little. "Why didn't you tell me?"

"Tell you what?" I ask. Oh no.

"You didn't tell me either," Dillon spills. His eyes don't meet mine. "You only told Ashley. Why did you only tell her?"

"She earned an answer."

"And we didn't?" May asks. Her eyes are staring at me like I'm crazy.

"She didn't want you guys to worry," Ashley answers.

"We wouldn't," they both say.

"Yes you would. May, you would be crying and showing her your puppy-dog eyes. And you Dillon would hold her tight and never let her go. She did it because she knew it was the only way to forget. She did what she had to."

"So *you* didn't freak out?" Dillon asks, accusingly.

"I did," Ashley admits. "But I knew she was going to be okay.

"I'm going to get you a drink of water," Ashley changes the subject.

She pulls May's arm along with her. When they leave the room, quietness fills up the space.

"I'm sorry you have to spend you Christmas Eve in a hospital," I say.

"It's okay. I was going to spend it with you anyways," he said. "Are you sure you're alright?"

I smile and nod. "I'm fine. Thank you for being here."

"I will always be here for you." He leans over and kisses me on my cheek. I try not to blush. "I'll tell your parents you're awake."

He leaves the room.

I loudly sigh and close my eyes. I think.

A glass cup of water appears on the nightstand.

Oh yeah.

I still got it.

CHAPTER 20

3 weeks later

I jump out of *my* new BMW and skip (not literally) into Shelly's office.

Over the past few weeks, everything changed almost automatically.

Jamui got a girlfriend. She's pretty, like all his girlfriends are. He talks a lot more now, hangs out with his friends, and smiles. He's graduating this year and going to UC Davis to be a mechanical engineer.

Saultan got a counselor for his nightmares. She helps him through it all. He doesn't have them much now, maybe three times a week, if even that. Also, he doesn't cry over them.

Islamiat is acting in school now. Everyone says she's really good. Of course, she likes the attention. I've only seen one of the plays she acted in and, to be honest, I liked it. She has talent.

I couldn't sleep in my bedroom anymore. I didn't want to. Not when I knew that someone very special to me had died on that carpet. I could still smell her in that room and see her body on the ground. I was put in a new room and I tried to forget about the sight.

Altogether, Ike had murdered seventy-eight children and five adults. Seventy-eight gifted kids and five innocent adults. I was given a medal from the president. It was given to me on national T.V.! It's an award for helping the cops capture the most wanted criminal in the United States. Even though I killed him instead of capturing him, it was said that the death penalty was going to be tossed at him anyways. But secretly, I knew he'd be able to get away. With the power we have, with the power more than two hundred kids have, we could probably save ourselves from the end of the world safely.

On Christmas, my whole family and I visited Erika's grave. We left beautiful, pink carnations around her resting place. I left a note that said I love you. I know she must already know that, but it still felt great to leave it on her grave.

Two days after that is Ms. Bell's funeral. There was police officers lined all along the walls. It reminded me of the hallway in Suzette Morales' house. Only, more people we're crying and there were flowers and prayers and no smoke or cheap perfume. My family didn't come. I told them they don't need to and, I don't know why, but I didn't really want them there. It's not like they knew her much anyways. But they helped get me ready and whispered a few prayers for her themselves.

I dressed in black and rode with Shelly. Like always, she looked stunning even with the wet eyes and red cheeks and raven colored dress. She wore a hat and low heels. We sat near the back while in the front Ms. Bell's two sons slumped in their seats, heads down, eyes hollow. Dr. Jeff came too. He sat beside me, said nothing with a nice suit on and no glasses. It was almost as depressing as Erika's funeral.

Then there's Malcolm. I was hardly alive when they got me on an ambulance that night, but Malcolm was even more gone. He didn't have enough blood to keep him going, so there was low hope. But Shelly screamed in their faces and they raced him to the hospital as fast as they could. They gave him all the attention they could offer. And the next morning, he opened his eyes.

I was released from the hospital sooner than he was. I visited when I was able to. Shelly was there each time, reading a book or writing something in her journal while Malcolm slept. The blinds were kept wide open, and if Shelly fell asleep, her head would lay on the bed with Malcolm's hand in her hair.

Out of the nine times I visited, he was awake only four times. Whenever he saw me walk in, he'd call out, "Here comes in a hero". I've never been called a hero before, so I always looked away and smiled. But he'd grin, sit up, and tell me how brave and stubborn I am. His hand would be closed around Shelly's, his stomach bandaged, and I'd think to myself, you're a hero too.

"Morning Amy," I greet Shelly's assistant.

"Oh, morning Miss Wilson," she nods at me. "Mrs. Clark is waiting for you."

"Thanks."

When I get close to her door, I can hear chattering inside. I knock once, lightly. There's a laugh on the other side and Shelly raises her voice to shout, "Come in!"

I open the door and step inside. I rearrange the blue scarf, the one given to me by Ms. Bell.

Shelly's behind her desk, sitting in her seat with her elbows on the top and hands hooked together. Her hair is down and flowing to her waist. The green in her eyes sparkle, like when the sun's reflecting hits the ocean, while the blue on the sidelines try to gain some spotlight. She grins when she sees me walk in, lugging her eyes off of Malcolm's face.

He's half-way sitting on the opposite side of her desk, one leg dangling in the air and the other one resting on the floor. He still winces when he moves too fast, but he's up and running, taking care of his work and, when he's not busy, flirting with Shelly.

In his hands he's playing with an accessory from Shelly's desk, a light, iron ball with designs over the top. He rolls it in his fingers and lets it go, catching it in his other hand. When I walk in, he throws the ball in the air and captures it with his left hand.

"Here comes in a hero," he announces.

"Are you always going to say that?" I question.

"Until it gets old."

Shelly rolls her eyes.

"How's everything?" she asks.

"Great," I nod with my answer.

"So, what's up? Why make an appointment?"

I didn't expect Malcolm to be present, but I'm even gladder he is.

"I have a proposal," I said.

"What for?"

I take a deep breath. I lock eyes with Shelly's because I want her to know that I mean what I'm about to say.

"To make a school. Well, boarding school. For kids like me."

Shelly's mouth slightly falls open.

Malcolm lets out a chuckle. "Kids like you? Please define to me what about you there needs to be a school for."

I look at him, wondering and suggesting. Then I open my hand and a pair of sunglasses appears. A boring pair but Malcolm's jaw falls and his blue eyes expand.

Shelly gets out of her chair and pushes his mouth shut. "You said you wanted to know."

He finds his way to move and takes the sunglasses from my hands.

"So this is how he did it," determines Malcolm. "Magic."

"Nope," I say. "It's more like…a mental ability. It all comes from here," I point at my head. "It's very powerful. If you screw around with it, it will attempt to kill you."

"Is that how you got him?" he looks up at me.

"Yes."

I think his eyes are screaming "Murderer!" or "Killer!" but all Malcolm says is, "Smart."

"I don't know Miss Wilson," Shelly said, leaning on her desk beside Malcolm. "Where will we put it? Who'll pay for it? Who will teach them?"

"I'm sure Malcolm can help find a place for it," I said. "Leave the money up to me. I'll pay for the making of the building."

"And teaching? School's *need* teachers."

"It's true our best teacher is gone now," I said, bowing my head for Ms. Bell, "but there's still Dr. Jeff and me. And you too, Shelly. After that, I'm sure Dr. Jeff has other friends he can trust and teach them as well."

"*Me*? You want me to teach something I know nothing about?"

"That's not true. You'd be a great teacher. You taught me a lot."

She smiles.

Malcolm puts the sunglasses on. "A school for the gifted. The president's going to think we're on crack."

"Will he have to know?" I ask.

"It will make it easier to run it," said Shelly. "And if you're serious about this, maybe it would be a good idea to bring you along to tell him yourself, sense you are proof."

I am, aren't I?

"How will you find the kids that are like you?" ask Malcolm.

"Their DNA. And that notebook you retrieved from Ike's warehouse. There are over a hundred names on there of kids that are still alive."

"What grade would you like to start at?" said Shelly. "Sixth grade?"

I stop to think first. "My sister had a hold on her gift when she was only three years old. We're starting at first grade."

"This is amazing," says Malcolm. "You're really going to do it?"

"Yes. And I wouldn't mind to have a couple of trustworthy guards around the property."

"I go where Shelly goes," he says and takes Shelly's hand into his.

"Then I guess you're goanna help make this school a reality," she said, sliding in closer.

"I guess so." The glasses disappear of his face and he leans in for a kiss. The agent kisses him back.

I clear my throat. "So, are we all together on this?"

"I'll make some calls," agrees Malcolm.

"And I'll tell Dr. Jeff," said Shelly. "He'll be jumping with joy to help. Also, I'll get the list for you. But it's your job to get those kids to come."

"I'm fine with that." And I know just who to start with. She likes cake mix ice cream and skipping along with her dead grandma.

"You're an outstanding young lady Miss Wilson," Shelly said.

"Please, call me Mariam."

We share a smile. Before stepping out of the office, I turn to Malcolm, smiling a little.

"By the way," I say to him, "you might want to write down a note about the sunglasses I just made."

His eyebrows slide close together. "Why?"

"Just do it."

Shelly laughs and pats his cheek. He reaches out and catches her around her waist, pulling her to him. She shoves playfully at his chest, them both completely forgetting about me. I shut the door.

I get outside and walk through the parking lot to my car. I smile at nothing special and just think, things are going to get a lot better. Because everything is soaring just the way it's supposed to. I mean, I'm about to go meet my boyfriend, ex-best friend, then came back to be my friend and now we're a couple. Tomorrow, I'm back to school. After my teachers learned why I was failing my classes, they're allowing me to retake tests and turn in missing assignments. Even Mrs. Olden .Then after I get through school, volleyball practice (the coach decided to put me on the team because they know they can't win without me).

I climb in my car and shut the door. The engine comes alive and I jump onto the road. I go forward.

Forward is the only direction I'm going to go. I went forward in the woods.

I’m going forward now.

Made in the USA
Charleston, SC
20 July 2014